Money Hungry

A Salt Mine Novel

Joseph Browning Suzi Yee

Published by Expeditious Retreat Press
Cover by J Caleb Design
Edited by Elizabeth VanZwolle

For information regarding Joseph Browning and Suzi Yee's novels and to subscribe to their mailing list, see their website at https://www.joseph-browning.com

To follow them on Twitter: https://twitter.com/Joseph_Browning

To follow Joseph on Facebook: https://www.facebook.com/joseph.browning.52

To follow Suzi on Facebook: https://www.facebook.com/SuziYeeAuthor/

To follow them on MeWee: https://mewe.com/i/josephbrowning

By Joseph Browning and Suzi Yee

The Salt Mine Novels

Money Hungry	*Vicious Circle*
Feeding Frenzy	*High Horse*
Ground Rules	*Fair Game*
Mirror Mirror	*Double Dutch*
Bottom Line	*Dark Matter*
Whip Smart	*Silent Night*
Rest Assured	*Better Half*
Hen Pecked	*Soul Mates*
Brain Drain	*Swan Song*
Bone Dry	*Deep Sleep*

Chapter One

Boston, Massachusetts, USA
3rd of December, 1:23 p.m. (GMT-5)

Charles Winston Roberts rapidly paced the stairs of his six-story brownstone in an endless loop. As soon as he reached the bottom, he started for the top all over again. Up, down, up, down, up, down. As he reached the sixth floor for the seventh time, the monitor on his wrist beeped at him, warning him that his heart rate was too high. He was exhausted and buried under a mountain of sweat, but he knew what would happened if he stopped. If he surrendered.

He furiously pulled off the band and threw the small machine against the pristine lavender plaster wall. It left a small dent before falling to the floor with a thud that he couldn't hear over his bellowing breaths. The alarm fell quiet, like the rest of the house. His sneakers squeaked as he abruptly pivoted for another pass—his stride frantic, his eyes wild.

In other circumstances, Roberts cut a dashing figure at six feet two, toned, and tanned. His tousled auburn hair and a playful smile hinted at the rogue he had been in his youth, while his face and demeanor displayed the distinguished patina men didn't develop until later in life. Normally, there was an effortlessness about him, cultivated over a lifetime of privilege and brilliance.

Roberts may have hailed from Harvard but unlike the other trust funders, he'd wanted to be and do something substantial. By his reckoning, the world didn't need more bankers or lawyers; it needed visionaries. Accordingly, he'd gone into medicine, and in the course of study, found his passion in pharmacology. There was something almost tactile to how proteins folded and found their receptors, like microscopic origami. He'd finished his MD but instead of going into practice, he immediately dove into creating new medications to correct aberrant physiologies with ardent abandon.

Mementos of his career lined the stairwell; he'd passed them so many times that they no longer registered in his conscious mind, even though they marked his journey. They were like highway mile signs—always there, but no one paid attention to the actual numbers until they were looking for their exit.

On the sixth-floor landing, between a raging Canadian landscape by Paul Peel and a peaceful Brazilian landscape by Frans Post, resided his first chemical patent. Fibroxocam, the first fourth-generation calcium channel blocker, was the first drug to generate more than a billion in revenue that didn't come out of the R&D department of one of the major pharmaceutical companies—an accomplishment tactfully understated by the simple oak frame.

His second patent graced the third-floor landing. Robixinol was a third-generation sulfonylurea lacking the negative pancreatic effects of the prior generations, and it held a special place in Roberts's heart. Not only did it dismiss any claims that Fibroxocam was a fluke or stroke of luck, it was the first patent awarded to his newly formed company Detrop Pharmaceuticals. Formerly Blandon Generics, he'd purchased it using the profits from Fibroxocam and restructured the company from one that only made generic medications to a first-rate enterprise with a robust R&D division. Now, it was one of the top fifty pharmaceutical companies in the world.

Hanging next to the Robixinol patent was his first *Time* cover, earned after he relinquished his patent on Fibroxocam. His CFO had fought him tooth and nail on the decision, but Roberts stood firm. The calcium-channel blocker had done well for him, and it was time to open it up and make it affordable to people who couldn't pay for the brand name. He'd eventually sold the idea as an advertising and marketing expense that would be offset by sales of the generic version from their own manufacturing facilities. With the increase in people using the medication and having a head start on generic production, it was a numbers game the CFO was willing to play to keep Roberts happy.

His most-recent *Time* appearance hung above the last steps leading to the ground floor. The main cover line read "The Johnny Appleseed of Pharmaceuticals?" underneath Roberts's beaming face. It was a valid supposition after he'd released his sixth patent into the generic market four years ago.

Roberts was intent on climbing the stairs once again, but his heart and lungs forbade it. He had to pause, boring his eyes into the thick mahogany double doors that kept out the noise of late-lunch traffic. He mentally did the math: he'd done seventy flights of stairs in one go.

Although fit, it wasn't something he'd planned on...but after his last episode, he'd vowed that he'd never lose control again. Five times he'd succeeded in pushing the craving into a dark pit where it could not see the light of day, but it gnawed at him, like a dog trying to get the last bit of meat off a bone. No matter how much he starved it, it wouldn't die. It only got hungrier.

When he caught his breath and his heart rate slowed to merely racing, Roberts again felt the yearning from which he'd been running. He dug deep for resolve but had nothing left. He was so tired of resisting. Instead of climbing the stairs one more time, he staggered to the Heppelwhite sideboard for his keys and reached for the polished wooden doors.

It was a typical early December day in Boston, and the sky was thick with clouds threatening to spill into a light drizzle at any moment. Even though the cold blasted through the doors, Roberts was unaware of the chill. Dressed only in a t-shirt and sweatpants, he exited northeast along Commonwealth Avenue on foot, weaving through the foot traffic on the sidewalk before crossing over to the greenbelt median. After a few minutes, he passed into the Boston Public Gardens and then into Boston Commons. The trees had lost their charm and stood like bundles of toothpicks amid the sad grass awaiting the impending onslaught of winter's snow.

Roberts didn't see the gawkers staring at his lack of a jacket as he jogged along the downtown streets. He didn't hear the cries of people he bumped into when they stepped in his way. He just ran, and the will to fend off his desires was sucked into that black hole shared by all junkies. He was no longer running away from something but toward it, and all that mattered now was satisfying his singular need.

*****

The ding of the door alarm took the owner of Massachusetts Coin and Bullion by surprise. The lunch rush, if you could call it that, had ended half an hour ago, and he usually spent the subsequent two hours of dead time reading archeology, history, and finance articles related to his business. He looked up from his tablet and took off his readers; he was an older man, nearly elderly if he was being honest about it, but still "sharp as a tack," as his granddaughter was fond of saying.

His visitor was male, well over six feet according to the security camera height strip, although it was hard to tell as his hair was unruly enough to add a few inches. He wasn't dressed like his regular customers and was breathing heavily, as if he'd just finished a run; again, something which his normal customers did not do. His typical customers were older, mentally inquisitive, and rather rotund, much like himself.

He put on a polite smile and greeted the potential customer on the other side of the counter. "How can I help you?"

The puffing man walked directly to him. "I'd like to buy some Maple Leafs, please."

"Any particular condition or year?" he asked, getting up from his chair.

"It doesn't matter, as long as they're pure gold," the sweaty man replied.

"Don't have to worry about that. They are the purest gold coins on the market. Made by the Royal Canadian Mint from gold mined exclusively in Canada," he added authoritatively.

The corners of the customer's mouth almost lifted into a smile as he nodded, and for a second, the owner thought he looked familiar. Was he one of the local bankers he passed on his trip from the parking lot to his store? He tried to imagine him cleaned up and in a suit, but he couldn't stretch his imagination that far.

"You a collector?" he chewed the fat, hoping to coax the face out of his memory with a little small talk.

The man didn't meet his gaze or answer his question right away. Instead, he pulled out his wallet—a walnut brown leather affair with white thread stitching and "Hentley" written upon the side. *An awfully nice wallet…too nice for sweatpants and a t-shirt*, the owner commented to himself. "Not particularly," he finally answered. "Whatever you have in stock will be fine."

*Ah, an investor…*he neatly categorized his customer. "I just got in the last shipment of this year's mint. How many would you like?"

The man held his wallet open, as if in a trance, before saying, "A dozen. I'd like a dozen, please."

The owner hesitated for the briefest second; he wasn't one to turn away business, but something didn't sit right about the request or the customer. Was it some sort of a scam? He'd seen an online video last week about a pickpocket who could steal the timepiece off your wrist while chatting with you. Or maybe he was just buying it with someone else's money? He'd signed up for an instant background service a few years ago to ensure that he didn't get involved with criminals. He rarely used it, but he'd gotten his money's worth the few times he felt the need to.

"That's a rather sizable purchase. I don't take checks or cash for such a large amount," he said emphatically.

"That's fine. I'll be paying by credit card," the man affirmed, passing the card over the counter.

"I'll need a driver's license as well," the owner added. "And I may have to call the credit card company to verify funding. Just to make sure everything's on the up and up, you know?"

"Of course." The man's fingers fumbled under the owner's watchful eye. He scrutinized every movement until he had the man's driver's license in his hand. He examined the picture; it seemed to match the face. Then he checked the name on the credit card against the ID: Charles W. Roberts.

It triggered a memory and the owner let his guard down. "Thank you, Mr. Roberts. I won't need to call the card company—I know you're good for it." He returned the license with a smile. "Let me get your coins and process the payment. It'll be just a second."

Roberts nervously drummed his fingers against his thigh while he waited. It took every ounce of concentration to keep from fixating on the rows of beautiful coins beneath the thick Plexiglas case. When the old man returned, he tried to make conversation with Roberts. "You know you saved my life? That's what my doctor said. Couldn't get my blood pressure under control until I started taking your medicine..."

Roberts absentmindedly nodded as the shopkeeper blathered on. He rapidly signed the charge slip as soon as it was set in front of him. When the man behind the counter handed him a boxed roll of twelve fresh-from-the-mint Maple Leafs, he reverently cradled it in his arms. An explosive laugh brought Roberts back to the present, and he registered the old man's voice again, "...but we're all getting older and every prescription adds up, don't you know."

"Do you have a restroom I could use?" Roberts nearly slurred his words. "It's a long jog back home."

"Certainly, certainly!" the shopkeeper replied. "Just go

through the doors there. It's on the right."

Roberts made his way to the back and ripped open the box once he was on the other side of the door. He took the first coin in his hand, and an electric shiver ran through his entire body as its cold weight pressed against his palm. It felt like the first time a man had gently run his fingers across his naked stomach.

He almost slipped up, but caught himself when he noticed a small security camera in the corner. He forced himself to wait for gratification and stumbled into the bathroom, where there shouldn't be any cameras. And there weren't.

When Roberts exited the Massachusetts Coin and Bullion a few minutes later, its owner enthusiastically waved goodbye and wished him a good day. In the shopkeeper's opinion, he looked a bit more composed, but he was still a far sight from the magazine covers. *That's what people really look like without all that hair and makeup*, he mused as he settled back into his chair.

He swiped his finger across the tablet and picked up where he left off. Apparently, a pair of plucky metal detectorists just discovered the second-largest Anglo-Saxon hoard in England last month. He sighed wistfully; he'd love to find something like that. As a lifelong numismatist, he held a deep affection for all manner of coins and the metals from which they were traditionally made. Whenever he had a coin in his hand, he was acutely aware he was holding a piece of history.

Chapter Two

Detroit, Michigan, USA
7th of December, 6:04 a.m. (GMT-5)

The morning was cold, dark, and silent. The first snow of the season had fallen silently during the night, coating the city in a thin layer of white. It was enough accumulation to bring much of the country to a halt, but it didn't faze the residents of Michigan, who would no doubt comment on its late arrival—but better late than never. The blare of engines firing up broke the reverent calm as the Postal Service morning fleet departed their massive Detroit distribution center. They had miles go to before it was time for dinner with their families at the end of the day.

David Emrys Wilson woke to the rumble and reached for the alarm clock on his night stand, switching it off before it had a chance to buzz. He never needed it in his fourth story loft thanks to the predictability of the U.S. Postal Service, but he still set it, just in case. He hated being late, even for work.

Wilson rose from the warm bed and took stock of the weather with a quick peek at the window. The thermometer on the window read 6° F and there was a slight frost around its exterior corners. He grinned at the healthy dusting before as he started his morning calisthenics. He loved the way the soft white blanket tempered his industrial landscape for a good four—if not more—months out of the year. And unlike the snow on the streets, the rooftop powder kept its clean color throughout the season and brightened his loft as it reflected the weak sunlight. Not that he would be there to appreciate it; he would be out the door before the sun fully rose and still at work when it set.

He started with jumping jacks, unconcerned about the noise it would make. Not only was he the sole person living in the building, it was the only residence in the area except for some apartment buildings on Fort and Lafayette. It had taken a lot of charm—and a little bit of graft—at the zoning board, but he knew nothing if not how to work the system. 500 10th Street was officially the only single-family residence in the light industrial neighborhood along the Detroit River just west of downtown, and within nine months of closing, property renovations were in full swing.

It had taken a lot of careful consideration to alter the existing structure to his needs. The brick and tile warehouse was built in 1868 for the Detroit Cast Iron Stove Company, and for the next sixty-four years, it held stack upon stack of iron stoves. After the company failed in 1932, the warehouse stood empty for twenty years before being put back into service for a series of companies associated with the auto industry. When that bottomed out in the late 1980s, the warehouse was vacant for a while until it was purchased by the Thailand Import Company. On paper, they brought in a variety of trade goods from all over Southeast Asia, but mostly they just imported heroin. After the drug bust in the 2010s, the warehouse was abandoned again until Wilson picked it up for a song.

Its renovated state would have endlessly intrigued guests, were Wilson one to have visitors. The four-story warehouse circumscribed 8,000 square feet, and the first thing he did was section off a floor on the upmost level. The actual living area was a modest 1,000 square feet, with all modern conveniences; the rest of the space was set aside for more esoteric needs.

The top floor was accessed through a restored wrought-iron spiral staircase inlaid with beautiful silver designs that few in the world would recognize, much less understand. Adjacent to the staircase was an old fireman's pole inscribed in a similar manner. He never knew when he would need a fast escape.

But the remodeling didn't stop there. He'd arranged for a number of security measures. All the first- and second-floor windows were bricked up, and the windows of the upper two floors were updated and their panes replaced with bulletproof glass. He had an inverted talus wall built—ten feet thick at its base that narrowed to a single foot twenty feet above the ground. A pound of powdered silver, iron, copper, and salt was mixed into each batch of reinforced concrete strong enough to resist any firearm that wasn't artillery. The only opening in the curtain of concrete was a massive six-ton steel garage door. Wilson had paid the contractor a ten percent bonus to do as he was told and not ask questions—as long as it wasn't illegal, it wasn't his business.

A different contractor installed a hanging catwalk along the third-floor windows to give him an unencumbered 360-degree view of the perimeter. He too got a bonus for his silence, but he wasn't as good at keeping his word as the first contractor. Fortunately, Wilson always took precautions. When the contractor went to tell his closest friend about the strange job he'd just finished, he found that he didn't really want to say anything about it. It felt akin to talking about the small caring things his wife did for him: something he would never share with anyone. Something to cherish and take with him to his grave.

After Wilson finished his last set of push-ups, he felt the warm rush of endorphins spread through him. He was a small, trim man just shy of five and a half feet, fastidious in maintaining his fitness. The few pounds he'd added since his graduation from Camp Peary more than two decades ago were pure muscle, only achieved through increasing his protein intake after exercise. Getting slow and doughy was ill-advised because of his work, which was rewarding but dangerous, as evidenced by the handful of scars he bore. Most were standard fare for one in his profession, except for one particularly bad cluster on his left side stretching from back to abdomen. It looked like a bear had mauled him, which was preferable to what had actually attacked him all those years ago.

His shower was short, but that didn't stop the mirror from steaming up. He ran an electric razor over his face and wiped a towel over the mirror. His intense brown eyes inspected his work and found it acceptable. Back in his bedroom, he reached into his double-sized armoire for a heavy winter suit: a charcoal gray herringbone with a starched white shirt and azure silk tie.

As he tightened the tidy Windsor knot, the smell of coffee wafted in from the kitchen. Like clockwork, his automated double-cup was waiting for its lid, but not before he added a touch of sugar and cream. Cup in one hand, Korchmar Monroe attaché in the other, he descended the spiral staircase.

His Porsche 911 was waiting for him on the ground floor, and he put his briefcase on the leather passenger seat before sliding into the driver's seat. He never locked his car at home; it was the one lapse in security he indulged in. The 500, as he referred to his home, was impenetrable to ordinary burglars looking to steal something as trivial as a car.

The engine purred to life and the massive solid steel garage door lifted, releasing a blast of cold air into the warehouse. He pulled outside and waited to leave until he verified the garage door was fully lowered. It reminded him of the upper jaw of some giant animal as the teeth of the door locked into the reinforced concrete ground.

Wilson eased onto the street, cautiously testing the pavement for ice. They should have salted the roads to keep ice from forming, but he never took anything for granted. Finding traction on the solid pavement, he gained speed and set off southwest along West Fort Street for the four and a half mile drive to Zug Island, home of the Salt Mine.

Zug Island was created in 1888 when Samuel Zug, a bookkeeper who made his fortune selling furniture, allowed the River Rogue Improvement Company to dig a channel along the south side of his property, turning the marshy peninsula into an island. The subsequent canal straightened the final precipitous curve of the river, making it more accessible for shipping. Later, Henry Ford would expand the same waterway to accommodate even larger vessels. When Zug sold the island for three hundred thousand dollars in the 1890s, it was the largest real estate deal of its day, but it ended up only being used as a dumping ground for various industries.

However, Zug Island was destined for greater things, starting with Detroit Iron Works, which purchased the island a decade later. They'd cleaned it up and built a pair of the largest blast furnaces in the world. While they were pumping out tremendous quantities of pig iron, a portion of the island was sold in 1911 to Discretion Minerals. Their interest lay in the massive salt layers formed during the Devonian Period four hundred million years ago when the salt waters of the Michigan Basin evaporated and the land uplifted. The mineral company didn't hit paydirt until it had dug eleven hundred feet through the rocky ground that sat beneath the marsh. Salt started flowing out of the mine a year later, and hadn't stopped in more than a hundred years, even after Discretion Minerals was acquired by the CIA for part of the MKULTRA project in 1955.

With its innate seclusion, Zug Island was an ideal site for operations. It was separated from the rest of the Detroit Metro Area and only had two occupants—one needed to be an employee of one of the two businesses to even get onto the island. The CIA had beefed up security and added a few more technological protections, but the real gem was the wandering nature of the mine, easily amenable to sectioning. After a few years, most of the real salt workers were unaware that anything covert was occurring. The CIA counted on people not knowing the true extent of the mines—more than 1,500 acres—as part of the site's protection, and whenever additional space was needed, it was simply carved out of the earth and carted to the surface as more production.

With light traffic, Wilson made to the island in less than ten minutes. He pulled up to the guard station and exchanged some pleasantries with the guard as he presented his cover ID: Davis Watson, Director of Acquisitions. Mondays were always the same. "Ya have a good weekend?" or "Didja catch that game?" Wilson wasn't one for chitchat, but he always nodded, if tersely at times.

Once he was waved through, he drove to the western part of the island and descended into a belowground parking complex. He parked, set his car alarm, and entered the elevator after waiting a few moments to ensure he would be alone. A quick flick of a titanium key and the elevator descended to a secret floor, what those in the know called the first floor of the Salt Mine.

"Good Morning, Wilson," the chipper mechanical voice of Angela Abrams rang out before the doors fully opened.

"Morning, Abrams," Wilson responded. Abrams sat opposite the elevator behind a layer of ballistic glass thick enough to stop a grenade. Her voice was piped in via a rather old speaker in the top corner of the otherwise barren metal room. "Buzz me in?"

"You never stop trying, do you?" she chided with a chuckle and a slot opened on the left wall. "Put your weapon and briefcase inside, please." Wilson deposited his Glock 26 and attaché. The sliding door closed and mechanical noises could be faintly heard through the steel.

"Do anything special over the weekend?" Abrams made small talk. The scan would take a minute—a battery of assessments was occurring.

"I watched a documentary about the history of World War I tanks."

"Not what I'd consider special, but to each their own," she tactfully replied. "I finally got to try out Grey Ghost, and it was wonderful."

Wilson nodded, although he wasn't much of a restaurant person. "I've heard good things about it."

"It was spectacular," Abrams tinned through the speaker. "You should go. Bring someone with you and make a night out of it," she suggested.

"If the situation ever arises, I'll remember the tip," he answered noncommittally. Thankfully, the machine beeped and he was buzzed in, sparing him any more conversation about his private life. He preferred it remain that way—not only because of his natural introversion, but because the less anyone knew about him, the safer he was. Information was power and the world was filled with the unscrupulous.

Once he was on the other side of the entry, he reached for his gun and felt its familiar contour in his hand as he holstered it. He'd vacillated for a full month between the 26 and the 43 before deciding that the increased magazine capacity justified the slightly larger profile. Firstly, because he had a good tailor to adjust his suits to maintain concealment, and secondly, the difference between six and ten rounds could be a matter of life or death when it came to his quarry.

With his case in hand, he walked through the stark entryway and down a long metal corridor to two elevators that went deeper into the earth. Wilson took the one on the left, opening it with a scan of his palm. The one on the right had no scanner and only provided access to the four topmost levels of the Salt Mine. The left side communicated with six floors, of which he had access to the top five. He'd been to the sixth floor many times, but it was only accessible to Leader, her two assistants, the librarians, and the armorer. The sixth floor was a mishmash of storage and workshops, but it was informally known as the Library, given the large number of unusual books held there.

Another palm scan, this time coupled with a retinal scan, delivered him to the fifth floor. In stark contrast to the spartan industrial design of the entry and elevator, the fifth floor was stylish in its own right. The structural elements of the large communal area were cut from the salt itself, and stark, angular ornamentations glittered under the multiple full-spectrum lights. Populated by black and white leather furniture, smooth clean lines drew the eye toward the sweeping ramps that led up to the rows of private offices. A gleaming silver tube containing the mechanicals streamed down the hall, itself dividing into dozens of argent snakes of progressively smaller size as it delved away from the elevator. In another setting, it could have been the cover story in an architectural magazine focused on Scandinavian design.

Although capable of comfortably holding dozens, the room was empty. Most of the rooms in the Mine were. At its peak in the 1950s, there had been nearly six hundred employees, but staff was now down to a little more than a hundred, of which only six were field agents like Wilson. There were two dozen empty offices on this floor alone.

Wilson ascended the salt ramp and walked down a corridor, flanked by thick metal doors bearing brass nameplates. As he passed each one, he subconsciously read the names on the doors. He'd known twelve of them personally in his years at the Mine. None of them had retired.

When he reached his office, the last on the left, another palm scan triggered the heavy chunk of his door's lock. He switched on the light, visually inspecting the space for signs of intrusion. Everything was as he left it, and he hung his coat on the thin Amish hall tree near the door.

Each agent was allowed to customize their office, provided they subjected everything to a rigorous testing and personally moved their furnishings. Wilson had chosen a 1935 Art Deco walnut desk, French-polished with rounded corners and twin locking doors. He'd paired it with a leather and walnut swivel chair of similar design. Getting them in had been difficult, but he'd managed with the help of one of his fellow agents for whom a twenty-five-year-old Laphroaig proved an adequate bribe. Opposite the desk was a single red-cushioned chair of no special make or quality. Its presence was more a formality than an invitation, which was consistent with Wilson's opinion of visitors in his office. The more-astute noticed and the contrary sat back nonetheless.

Behind the desk was a long row of darkly stained pine bookcases and filing cabinets—his personal collection of information. Everything here was a duplicate of something in the Library's stacks, but he found having a core collection of reference materials at hand useful. He always had access to his office and the same could not be said of the sixth floor.

He methodically put his things away in the shallow closet that contained his three pre-packed suitcases. Mentally labeled Hot, Cold, and Temperate, he kept them packed and ready. Should he be called away quickly, he liked to be prepared for changes in local climate. The last thing he put away was his cell phone; there would be little use for it here. Even his computer—a bulky black monstrosity that was screwed in place—wasn't connected to the internet. No line out to the greater world meant no one else could have a line in.

He sipped his still warm coffee as he looked though the in-basket on his desk. The first of the two thin files was a battered manila folder with OFFICIAL – SM EYES ONLY inked in black. It was on his desk every morning and elicited little interest. But the second was a green one bearing the bright red AGENT RESTRICTED – SM EYES ONLY: information designated for Salt Mine employees with agent-level clearance. It wasn't every day one of those was waiting for him.

He eased into his well-worn chair and flipped open the more intriguing folder, holding the edges with precision learned through repetition. After a minute of perusal, a single quizzical eyebrow marred his normally stoic face.

Chapter Three

Detroit, Michigan, USA
8th of December, 6:05 a.m. (GMT-5)

Wilson woke to the sounds of dozens of mail trucks rolling down his street but forwent his normal routine. He had an appointment, and he couldn't be late. In less than twenty minutes, he was dressed and on the road. Tuesday's guard wasn't as talkative as Monday's, and he was through the gate and into the parking garage without any obligatory pleasantries. He preferred Tuesdays.

Like normal, he reversed into his parking space—he never knew when he'd want to leave in a hurry—and waited in his car, darting his eyes off his phone whenever another vehicle entered the lot. He was looking for an octane red Dodge Charger rented to Teresa Maria Martinez. She had a seven o'clock appointment, and based on her file, Wilson assumed she'd show up early to get her bearings and ensure punctuality. There were no online photos of the interior of Zug Island, and it's what he would have done in her place. As expected, she rolled up at 6:42. Wilson exited his car when the tail of her

Charger cleared the entrance and waved her to park next to him. She complied.

Despite his outwardly indifferent appearance, Wilson was intently observing her, feeding the relentless assessment machine that constantly churned in his head. It was something good agents did—pay attention to every tiny detail without revealing such.

A moment later, the engine shut off and she got out of her car but left the door open. Martinez was tall, 5'10", and wide in the shoulders. Her face matched the photo in her file: shoulder-length brown hair the color of a stirred cappuccino and eyes that nearly matched. When she'd risen out of her Charger, her twill pants had tightened around particularly muscular thighs. He didn't have visual confirmation, but suspected the slight bulge on her side was her gun. She was FBI and allowed concealed carry.

"Mr. Watson?" she inquired before accepting his proffered hand.

"The same," Wilson confirmed, shaking her firm grip. "And you must be Agent Martinez. Is there anything you'd like me to help you with?" he volunteered.

"No, thank you," she declined politely before bending to collect her coat, a stylish leather affair that fit her well. "The weather's a lot different than Portland, I'll say that." She hoisted her bag on her shoulder and secured the car. The warm engine of the Charger had already started ticking as it cooled.

"Indeed it is," Wilson replied. "Shall we?" He indicated the elevators. As Wilson performed his titanium key routine, he caught Martinez watching out of the corner of her eye. She opened her mouth and was about to say something when he held up a finger. "We'll be able to speak freely in a minute," he explained as they descended.

"Good Morning, Mr. Watson," the chipper mechanical voice of Angela Abrams once again rang out before the doors had fully opened.

"Morning, Abrams," Wilson responded.

"I see we have a guest today. A Ms. Martinez, I believe?"

"You don't miss a thing," Wilson prosaically observed, already loading his attaché into the waiting metal slot while unholstering his Glock. He signaled that Martinez should do the same and she followed suit, depositing her bag and pulling her Glock 43 out from under her jacket. They tacitly approved of each other's weapon of choice.

"I watched that World War I tank documentary you mentioned yesterday. It was actually pretty interesting," Abrams said from behind the glass.

"I'd glad you gave it a shot," Wilson replied with genuine surprise. The Mine's gatekeeper was much more into entertainment and dining than military history. "Which was your favorite?" Normally, he didn't willingly participate in conversation, but he had to kill time somehow with twice as much to scan.

Abrams straightened up at the rare follow-up question. "I liked the German one that kinda looked like the sandcrawler from the Star Wars movies."

Martinez turned and coughed to stifle a laugh, but Wilson caught it. Thankfully, Abrams had not. "I think that one's the German A7V. There's only one left in the world. Somewhere in Australia, I believe," he informed her as the machine continued its operation.

Abrams shrugged. "I'm not sure if that was it, but there were a ton of soldiers riding on it in the picture they showed."

"If you found that interesting, you should check out a documentary on World War II tanks," Martinez joined the conversation. "There was a tank commander in that war named Abrams. In fact, our current main battle tank is named after him."

"Huh. You learn something new every day," she flippantly remarked when a ping sounded. Abrams looked down at her monitor and reported with a smile, "All's clear. Have a good day." The door buzzed and they passed through, picking up their belongings on the other side.

"Now that we're secure," Wilson spoke as they walked down the long corridor to the dual elevators, "welcome to the Salt Mine. I'm not sure how much you've been told about what we do, but if it's anything like what I was told before I joined, you know next to nothing."

Martinez smirked at the frank introduction. "Considering

the number of security hoops I had to jump through just to get to this point, I gathered as much. But this is one of the highest-level operative centers in the FBI."

"So you consider this a good career move for you?" Wilson quizzically asked. He watched her face mull over his question.

"I was at a point where a change needed to be made and this seemed promising," Martinez answered candidly without revealing much. Of this, Wilson approved.

"Would you still feel as enthusiastic about the position if I told you that we've lost a significant number of agents in the past four years?" he put it to her straight.

"I guess it would depend on the reason. Profession attrition is to be expected, but operational laxness, training failure, or lack of field support would be more concerning," she answered after giving it some thought. "Although, if the fallen agents were equally as methodical as you have been since our meeting, I would have to rule out inadequate training."

Wilson accepted the compliment with a slight nod and placed his palm on the scanner to summon the elevator. "Sadly, it's none of those things," he said bluntly. "What we do here is uniquely dangerous."

"Working as an FBI field agent isn't exactly a cushy desk job," she answered in stride, "and I keep my affairs in order."

"Right," he affirmed. "One of two daughters of a single parent, parents and sister now deceased. Everything goes to your sister's daughter Rose, adopted by a family in Colorado."

He watched for her reaction in his peripheral vision.

She flinched ever so slightly but quickly recovered. "It seems you are more informed about my situation than I am about the Salt Mine." The elevator doors opened and they entered in silence. Again, she paid close attention to the mechanical dance needed to move the elevator to the fourth floor. "You're serious about security," she commented once they'd started to move.

"This isn't the average FBI facility. It's designed to keep out unwanted guests and to keep in unwanted problems," he replied vaguely.

"This is a redacted black site?" Martinez guessed. She'd done her own digging on the FBI's Detroit office, but found no reference to the Salt Mine nor any type of retention facility in the area.

"Of a sort, but before I can fully explain the situation, we've got to meet the boss first," he cut off any further inquires. Martinez nodded but was caught off-guard; she was under the impression Watson was in charge.

The elevator doors opened to the fourth floor where the walls were chiseled out of the salt itself. The sparkling white had streaks of gray and black with the occasional red from other mineral impurities, but that wasn't what took Martinez's breath away. It was the piercing gray eyes of the short woman standing at the entrance.

She was no more than five feet tall and her short black hair was peppered gray. She wore faded blue jeans and a hand-knitted sweater vest over a checkered long-sleeved shirt a little worn at the elbows. Despite her small stature and casual attire, she had an undeniable air of authority, like the prow of a supertanker—anything that came before her moved aside or was crushed.

Her gaze bore into Martinez like a palpable force, and the seasoned FBI agent found herself tightening her abdominal muscles, as if preparing for a punch in the gut. Without a word, the petite figure stepped into the elevator, held up her hand and eye to the scanner, and pressed the button for the sixth floor. She gave Wilson a curt nod as the doors closed. When they were shut, Martinez noticed she'd been holding her breath the whole time and exhaled a little louder than she would have liked.

"That's the boss?" Martinez incredulously asked.

"That's the boss," he repeated it as a statement. "She does that to people. I'd say you'll get used to it, but it took me years."

Martinez chose her words carefully. "She doesn't look FBI."

"That's because she isn't. The Salt Mine is a joint operation between the FBI and the CIA, and Leader isn't really either," Wilson started filling in the blacks for the prospective new agent.

Martinez's brow furrowed at the statement. "FBI and CIA? That doesn't make any sense."

"We go where we're needed and we have whatever credentials are required for the jurisdiction at hand. We're even part of Interpol when necessary; that badge gets a lot of use." Wilson gave her a moment to process the information and continued, "Not quite the job interview you expected, is it?"

She shook her head slowly as the elevator finally slowed. "And what exactly does the Salt Mine do under the direction of Leader?"

"I know you must have a lot of questions, but it really will be easier to show you than to try to explain," he negotiated for patience as they finally arrived at the sixth floor. "If you'll follow me."

The elevator doors opened to reveal a dimly lit corridor cut out of the salt. It lacked the spectacular sparkle of the fourth floor, but the light twinkled in the thousands of crystalline edges, giving the subterranean passage the feeling of walking through a starlit night.

Martinez stepped out and the elevator shut behind her. A little ting sounded as it returned toward the surface; there was no place to go but forward. "How far down are we?" she asked as their steps crunched on the rough saline floor.

"426 feet, give or take," he answered, adding the qualifier as an afterthought. They took several turns in silence before coming upon a silvery arch etched from top to bottom with hundreds of sigils and ornate tracings linking each etching. It reminded Martinez of the kind of prop kids stood in front of for prom pictures: A Night Under the Stars.

Wilson passed under the arch and paused on the other side,

turning to watch Martinez as she stepped through. She wasn't sure what was supposed to happen, or if the fact that nothing happened was a good or bad thing. His resumed his stride and started talking while walking.

"We're heading into the Library and we'll likely meet our librarians, Chloe and Dot, on our way. FYI, they are conjoined twins; try not to gawk. They get enough stares when they're topside, and I'd rather they not get any here."

Long columns of bookshelves carved out of black-striated salt filled the room beyond. The ceiling, at least forty feet high, was supported by dozens of massive pillars. Filling the shelves were row-upon-row of books. They were almost exclusively leather-bound and untitled, and there was a special section designed for holding scrolls, codices, and non-traditional works. Martinez didn't recognize any of the few rare titles that cropped up on the sea of brown, but Wilson's pace didn't give her much time to browse. The aisle terminated at a sprawling wooden counter occupied by two women. Had she not been warned, Martinez would have thought they were simply sitting extremely close to each other while reading.

"Wilson!" Chloe exclaimed with a smile as they approached. Dot remained focused on her book, a thick work penned in red ink.

"Chloe, you just broke my cover," he sighed.

"Oh, whatever," she dismissed. "I assume this is the new agent?"

"Of course she's the new agent; everyone else here knows Wilson, so there's no other way you could have broken his cover," Dot disdainfully reasoned, looking up from her book long enough to give Wilson a brief wave.

"Would you behave?" Chloe scolded her dour other half. "It's called being polite."

Once they reached the wooden counter, Martinez had full view of the pair. They were conjoined at the torso down to the hip, broader than a single person but not quite as wide as two. Otherwise, they were separate individuals, with Chloe on the right side and Dot on the left. They were both dirty blondes with undeniably similar facial features despite the stark differences in how they choose to present themselves. If they were music, Chloe was pop and Dot was alternative.

"Nice to meet you both," Martinez greeted them, extending her hand. Chloe shook while Dot merely gave her a nod, figuring Chloe had the niceties covered.

"Has he done the whole 'OoOoO, so mysterious' routine?" Chloe inquired.

"I'm standing right here," Wilson protested.

"Shush, we're talking about you," she shot back. "So?"

"A little bit," Martinez hedged.

Dot snickered at the response, but it was Chloe that spoke, "He does that, but he's not doing it on purpose. It's just something that can't be explained, but it'll all make sense in a few minutes," she said reassuringly. "Just remember to keep your hands, arms, feet, and legs inside the ride at all times and you'll be fine."

"Will do…just like a roller coaster," Martinez said dryly.

The hint of sarcasm drew Dot out of her book. "Don't worry, if you can't handle it, you'll forget all about it anyway," she obliquely chimed in.

Wilson gave her a sharp look. *Don't scare her away.*

Relax, I'm just having fun, she smirked back before returning to her reading.

Wilson responded with a blatant wristwatch check. "We should get going. We have a lot to do today." He made his exit, beckoning Martinez to follow.

"Take care!" Chloe called out as they approached another silver arch on the opposite side of the reading counter. "He's grumpy today!" she said to her sister.

"Always is," Dot argued.

"I can still hear you," Wilson declared before crossing under the threshold.

"If you're Wilson, who's Davis Watson?" Martinez asked.

"Still me," he answered. "It's the alias I use for mundane stuff and getting to the office. Davis Watson is the Director of Acquisitions for Discretion Minerals. My real name's David Wilson."

Martinez held out her hand in an exaggerated gesture. "Nice to meet you. My real name is still Teresa Martinez." He didn't take the bait and shooed her into another elevator.

“How far down are we going now?” she asked as the doors closed.

This elevator had no scanners and Wilson simply pressed the bottom floor: level twelve. “Another 400 feet or so,” he replied.

“And what does the Salt Mine need to keep 826 feet under the ground, give or take a few feet?” she queried.

Wilson had been in her shoes and knew the kinds of questions she must have, but he brushed aside the urge to explain. “It’s easier to show you. Just stay behind me and do exactly as I say,” he instructed. “For your own safety.”

How reassuring, Martinez thought to herself as she put on her game face.

The elevator doors opened to another twinkling, low-lit corridor, only this time the sounds of gunfire and explosions rolled from down the hall. Martinez reflexively reached for her weapon and looked to Wilson, who appeared unconcerned. She stood down and followed him along the passage. As they neared, the sounds grew louder, and roiling beneath them was a hissing screech that reminded her of the sounds dying deer made on long ago hunting trips in the Colorado Rockies with her dad. The noise elicited no reaction from Wilson, and they proceeded into sonic dissonance, rounding the corner on a strange tableau.

In the middle of a forty-foot square room sat a large man on a ratty puce-colored couch from the 1970s. He was dressed in jeans and a black T-shirt, a thick pair of white socks on his feet. Opposite the sofa was a TV, its bright lights displaying the jerky first-person perspective of a war game. If he noticed their arrival, he didn't show it. His mouth was open, the source of the disquieting screech. Etched into the striated salt of the floor was a giant silver circle, from which lines radiated inward. The outer ring was at least eight inches wide and the interior rays about half that. Next to the couch was a cheap wooden table, upon which rested a small lamp and several piles of books. The chamber was otherwise empty.

"Furfur!" Wilson finally called out, barely audible over the noise. The man briefly took one of his hands off the controller to increase the volume. Wilson looked at Martinez and shrugged before opening the door of the nearby fuse box, tripping a fuse and cutting power to the TV.

"Good morning, Furfur," he said once the room was silent.

"I wouldn't know, unless you're here to let me out," the man snapped back, putting down the controller. His voice was lush and mesmerizing, like the feel of a tight velvet dress, but there was an underlying anger that came through loud and clear.

"You know it's never going to happen," Wilson replied to the petulant greeting.

"Never's a big word coming from you," Furfur retorted, rising from the couch and stepping toward them. Martinez had to fight the urge to take a step back. He was at least 6'6" and nearly a yard wide at the shoulders. "Who's the newbie?"

he questioned, the word sounding foreign in his throat. A disquieting sneer came over his face. "Come to show off your prize lion?"

With a slight flourish, Wilson introduce Martinez to the sole occupant of the twelfth floor. "Meet Furfur, a great earl of Hell."

Chapter Four

Hindon House, Buckinghamshire, UK
8th of December, 11:45 a.m. (GMT)

Detective Chief Inspector Simon Jones parked on the wet gravel driveway of Hindon House, a sprawling manse built in the late Georgian period but embellished by many traits traditionally considered Victorian. There were already several vehicles in the large driveway conducting their preliminary assessments, waiting for his arrival before fully processing the scene. He exited into a dreary misty rain, the quintessence of a late autumn English day.

Detective Constable Tull greeted him as he crossed the threshold. The much younger man was fairly new to the service, and in fit and trim fighting condition, a nice complement to DCI Jones who was in his late fifties and a little paunchy. Jones used his experience to zero in on the culprit, and Tull ran down those foolish enough to flee.

"What do we have?" Jones inquired in that professional tone Tull was striving to acquire.

"Looks like a murder—" Tull began before Jones

interrupted.

"Never start with the conclusion, DC Tull. Start with the facts," Jones reminded him.

"Yes, sir. The body's in the drawing room," he started again, leading Jones into the adjacent chamber. "The deceased is Carlmon Grollo."

Jones stopped midstride. "*The* Carlmon Grollo of Brockham Laboratories?"

"The same," Tull responded from the massive doorway, twice as tall as he was. He waved his arm broadly, taking in the entire house. "Obviously business has…had…been going well for him." He waited for the DCI before proceeding.

The first thing Jones noticed when he entered the drawing room, besides the body slumped against a couch leg, was the lack of paintings. Interspersed along the walls were several bright square and rectangular patches conspicuously outlined from the darkened smoke-stained wallpaper.

"Where are the paintings?"

Tull led Jones around one of the leather Chesterfields. Stacked against the back of the sofa were eight empty frames. "If you look at the edges, they appear to have been slashed out," the constable stated.

Jones nodded and put on his gloves, running his fingers around the remaining canvas. "The edges are rougher than I'd expect. Normally, thieves use a razor to release a canvas; maintains more of the value," he educated as he examined. "See how rough and jagged these edges are?"

Tull bent down and agreed with his DCI. "That's definitely not the work of a Stanley knife."

"No, it is not," the DCI concurred before turning to inspect the body. It was slumped, face down, and curled in a fetal position against the wooden leg of a white upholstered Georgian couch. "Nothing's been touched?"

"The cleaning lady found him here and gave him a shake, but once she realized he was dead, she fled to the kitchen and gave us a call. She's in the dining hall being interviewed by Tillerson. They should be finishing up shortly."

Jones nodded and bent down, putting two fingers on the carotid artery. The body was cold. "What's the ETA for Mr. Hicks?"

"We haven't been able to reach him, so I sent a constable to his office, with instructions to go to his house if necessary." Even hunched over and facing down, Tull could see the irritation spreading throughout the DCI's body.

"And how long ago was that?" Jones asked, rifling through the jacket pockets of the deceased.

"Twenty minutes. I'm thinking they should return in the next ten minutes or so."

Jones grunted noncommittally, but then voiced a little sound of intrigue. He rose, holding a pair of child safety scissors. "What would these be doing on the floor under the body?"

"No idea, sir," Tull responded, producing an evidence bag for his DCI. Jones dropped the scissors into the clear plastic bag.

As Tull sealed and labeled the evidence, Jones flipped through the wallet he'd retrieved. "Looks to be complete. All the cards are still here, and there's a few hundred pounds."

"The thieves were after the big ticket items," Tull postulated.

"That would be my take on it as well. No reason to grab the cards—they're traceable—and the cash has to be miniscule compared to the value of the paintings." Jones dropped the wallet into another evidence bag. "Do we have any information on family yet? Insurance policies with listed goods or beneficiaries?"

Tull sealed the bag and pulled out his notebook, reading aloud, "Carlmon Grollo; age fifty-eight; CEO Brockham Laboratories, the UK's eighteenth largest pharmaceutical company. Unmarried, twice divorced, most recently two years ago. Three children: Mark, thirty-five; Elizabeth, thirty-two; and Jack, seventeen. Jack attends King Edward's School."

"So, the spouses are probably out of the picture, but confirm their alibis anyway, as well as those of the children. I'd expected at least one young child. This makes the scissors even stranger."

Tull shrugged, taking notes. "Maybe a memento of when they were younger? What are your thoughts on possible cause of death?"

"Safety scissors make a strange memento," Jones said as he crouched down again, double-checking what he'd already observed. He liked to be thorough. "There's no visible blood, and I can't see any trauma from this position. Perhaps something will reveal itself once the bloody coroner gets here." He stood and removed his gloves. "All right, let's make a quick sweep through the rest of the house and then speak with the housekeeper. Name?"

Tull accessed his pad. "A Mrs. Linda Sharpe."

"Hopefully she's as her surname describes. Let's take a look at the exterior first, with the expectation that Mr. Hicks will be here by the time we've finished."

Tull silently followed. He hoped the coroner would arrive by then. Once his DCI entered "grump mode," as Tull privately termed it, he was there for the rest of the day. They went outside and circumnavigated Hindon House. It was a fine example of transitional architecture, well maintained, and recently refurbished in some sections. There were no signs of forced entry, nor any depressions in the foliage or humus of the flowerbeds. A shiny new BMW pulled up as they completed the last of the exterior assessment—the garage.

"Finally!" Jones exclaimed just before the car door opened.

"Hello! Sorry I'm late; had a meeting that simply couldn't be interrupted," Cyril Hicks apologized, shaking hands with DCI Jones. Hicks was a tall, lean man, graying at the temples, and could have easily been a poster child for an advertisement of the established class. He was an influential local solicitor elected to coroner a few years ago. Jones missed the days when coroners were medical practitioners rather than legal ones.

Jones said nothing, indicating that there was work to be done with a twist of his head. Tull relayed the basic information to the coroner as he approached the body. Hicks also commented on the missing paintings while he gloved up and turned the corpse over, confirming the deceased's identity. "That's old Grollo, all right. I had dinner with him last week."

"You knew the deceased?" Jones's voice seemed neutral, but Tull could hear the edge in it even though Hicks didn't.

"For a very long time; old school chums—Eton," Hicks explained. "We dined a few days ago…had a long discussion regarding estate planning. He was interested in acquiring more art."

"Did he have any heart troubles?" Jones asked after noting a lack of any injury.

"None that I knew of, but we'll check his records when we get him in. The boys should be here shortly with the transit. The autopsy should put us straight."

"We found a pair of safety scissors on him. Like a child's. Did he have any current lovers? Illegitimate children?"

Hicks was taken aback by such a suggestion. "I highly doubt it, but I certainly wouldn't know if such were the case." He gathered himself and continued, "I'll put the fire under the ME with this one and we should have results by tomorrow at the latest. He owes me some favors and I'll…are you listening?"

Jones had snapped on another pair of gloves and hovered over the body, closely examining the mouth. "There's something in there," he muttered. "See that fleck of blue color?"

"What? I didn't…yes, there's something there. Let me check it out." Hicks pried open the corpse's mouth and dislodged a long multi-colored piece of ragged cloth, held it up, and wondered aloud, "What could this be?"

Tull waited for the DCI to respond first, but he seemed baffled. "Sirs, I think it's a strip of a painting."

"What?"

"Flip it sideways. It looks like part of a painting. See, that's the shore of a lake, there are the rushes…"

"Damn if you aren't correct, constable," Hicks cried out. "That's part of William Holman Hunt's *Ophelia!* It should be hanging over the mantel there." He pointing above the fireplace, as if there was some confusion as to what "mantel" meant.

"Did he *choke* on a painting?" DCI Jones quizzically guessed, not quite believing the words coming out of his mouth. All three men were dumbstruck at the notion. "Get a bag, Tull." He nudged his constable out of his bewildered state.

As Tull bagged and tagged the strip, Hicks dug deeper in the throat of his old friend. Sure enough, he found three more, each deposited into their own bag.

"Just what the hell happened here, Detective Chief

Inspector?" Hicks demanded.

"I have no idea, but we're going to find out."

After a few minutes of ineffectual speculation, the van arrived and the late Carlmon Grollo, age fifty-eight, CEO of Brockham Laboratories, was escorted to an appointment with a medical examiner who would be equally puzzled at the findings. Hicks departed with the van and the body. As they drove away, Jones mused, "Did you note how Mr. Hicks didn't seem that put out when he initially found his old chum face down and dead in the drawing room?"

"I thought it strange," Tull responded.

"As did I, Tully my boy, as did I."

Chapter Five

Detroit, Michigan, USA
8th of December, 7:00 a.m. (GMT-5)

Furfur bowed to Martinez. "I'd come shake your hand, but I'm afraid you'll have to come to me." His voice sounded no different than before, but the weight of it was like a wall of water pushing against her back. Without thinking, she took a step forward. Wilson's arm shot out across her chest, and the mild impact was enough to jar her from Furfur's influence and regain her balance against the power of the request. She stopped, confused.

"What the..?" Martinez whispered.

"He has that effect," Wilson explained. Furfur laughed, full-teethed. "You need to watch yourself around him. He can be very convincing."

Martinez suddenly became very angry. "What the hell is going on here?"

Wilson put himself between Martinez and Furfur, knowing full well where the circle was in relation to himself. "He's a devil. He has magic in his voice that can make us acquiesce to his desires before we realize what we're doing. He used it on you because he wants you to cross the silver pentagram binding him here." Wilson pointed to the lines of silver etched into the floor. She hadn't put the shape together, but now it seemed obvious.

"There's no such thing as devils or magic," she objected. "What's really going on?" Her eyes darted around the room, fruitlessly searching for clues of a reasonable explanation for what just happened.

"It's always the same now, isn't it?" Furfur rumbled philosophically. "In the old days, they'd instantly believe. 'Hello, I'm an earl of Hell' and they'd run before you, fleeing for their lives. Today, they're always checking for hidden wires or mirrors. The world is in a sorry state."

"Tragic," Wilson dryly responded while grabbing Martinez by the shoulders and gently moving her a few steps back. "Come on, let's back up a little. Remember to stay a bit behind me."

In the few seconds it took to move back and rearrange themselves, the vacant panic in her eyes had cleared. Wilson had gone through the same process years ago, and he remembered what it felt like. It was like taking an unexpected lungful of frigid air.

"I'm fine now," she firmly stated, removing his hands from her shoulders. "I'm fine!" She looked around him at the towering Furfur standing calmly at the edge of the silver circle.

In the backlight of the dim table lamp, his eyes faintly flickered cerulean. She took another step back to demonstrate to Wilson that she was in control of her faculties…or so she'd later tell herself.

"I like this one," Furfur murmured appreciatively. "She's cute."

"That's enough!" Wilson ordered over his shoulder, cutting off the next probable line of manipulation. He double-checked that Martinez's eyes were still clear before turning back around. "Cut the crap, Furfur. You know the routine."

"I remember meeting you for the first time. You were nicer then," the devil coyly remarked.

"And you were hairier. Now, show time," Wilson insisted.

"And hornier, too," he chuckled. "But I do like this form." He toyed with Wilson, stretching out an arm and examining it like one would a new piece of clothing. "It's quite convenient."

"Not for me. Do the change."

"No. I'm not in the mood," Furfur refused.

"I don't care; you know the arrangement." Wilson had the look of a father trying to reason with a toddler. Martinez watched the verbal volley in disbelief but stayed behind him.

A wicked smile came across Furfur's face. "I do. You don't have the rights."

"Leader does," Wilson said with finality.

Furfur scoffed at the name. "Then make her come down here and do her own dirty work. I'm done talking to her dogsbody!"

Martinez felt the gravitas behind those words, except this time there was no compulsion, only pure spite. To her surprise, Wilson just laughed. "And you wonder why you're not feared anymore? Dogsbody?" He chortled again and delivered his next line in a nearly perfect Mid-Atlantic accent, "Hello? 1935 here, we want our slang back."

The intense wave erupted from Furfur under Wilson's mockery. "A sense of *humor*, Agent Wilson?" He stressed the word, as if it were distasteful. "That is refreshing. Like a talking dog or a chimpanzee that smokes. An *agent* with a sense of humor!"

Wilson said nothing but the air between them was charged. Martinez was certain she was missing layers to the interaction, but whoever the prisoner was, she had no doubt that he'd gleefully end Wilson's life.

"I'm still not doing it," Furfur eventually announced.

Wilson sighed and addressed Martinez. "Since he's in an uncooperative mood, let's make our exit." He turned to leave and then paused, pointing at the fuse box. "But before we go, would you be so kind as to flip the other breaker to the off position for me? I don't want to waste any of Leader's electricity on frivolous expenses."

Martinez nodded and opened the box. There were only two fuses, and Wilson had already flipped one.

"Fine!" Furfur growled as she reached toward the handle.

"Turn the other one back on, and let's get this over with." Martinez glanced at Wilson. He nodded yes and she flipped the other breaker up to the on position. Power returned to the TV and game console.

A happy little giggle came out of Furfur at the glowing return of his entertainment. "Come here, newbie. You're only a virgin once and I want to see your face when I do it."

"I'm quite content here," Martinez replied, certain that no matter what happened next, she'd rather be farther away than closer.

"As you wish," Furfur purred with a deep and courtly bow. His flesh rippled and shook as he rose, gliding into new forms and absorbing his clothing as it progressed. He gained height, adding another foot to his already impressive stature. Fur sprouted throughout, except on his back where glorious white wings appeared, spreading out to twice his height. His head shifted and horns erupted into a tall and multi-pointed rack, matching the ungulate form his face finally settled upon. His lower body matched his head, transforming into a bipedal deer.

It took all of Martinez's will to remain still during the process. Each change was accompanied by a silent screaming protest within, as if the very fabric of her being fought against what was occurring dozens of feet away, as if she was somehow physically connected to the creature beyond the circle. Each ripple, each change she felt within herself, and it felt wrong.

"I am the Hellish Great Earl Furfur, and I will not always

be in this circle, little one. Pray that you are dead before I am free," he proclaimed before releasing the screams of the dying deer she remembered from her youth. Multifarious tones and voices arose out of his throat; eventually Martinez couldn't restrain the oncoming darkness. As she fell, Wilson caught her before she hit ground, just as he'd once been caught.

"I do love it when they faint," Furfur preened, proudly engorged from Martinez's involuntary reaction. "You should leave now—unless you want to watch, of course," he teased with a suggestive lick of his lips.

The worst part was that Wilson was tempted. *Goddamn devils*, he thought, as he carried Martinez away.

*****

Martinez woke on the elevator ride up to the Library. Wilson's arms were solidly wrapped around her, surprisingly strong. This close, he smelled musky.

"Good, I'm glad you're awake," he cheerfully spoke, immediately releasing her as she bore her own weight. "You're heavier than you look."

"Fainting on a job interview…first time for everything, I guess," she muttered, exasperatedly smoothing out her clothes. As she moved, her muscles ached.

"It happens to everyone," he said flatly. "The human neurological system simply can't take its first exposure to aethermorphism without shutting down."

Her face was pale. "That's a big word meaning what exactly?"

"Devils work with the aether to—"

"There's no such thing as aether," she stated emphatically.

"Not as historically postulated, but there most certainly is aether, and you felt its effects," Wilson said as gently as he knew how. His attempt at softening the facts was disarming and her mind spun. *If devils and aether were real…*

"I feel like I hit the gym way too hard yesterday. My mouth's dry, and my hands feel clammy," she sidestepped the subject.

"It'll pass in an hour or so," Wilson reassured. "Drinking water helps." The elevator stopped and the doors silently opened, revealing the Library's central massive chamber. Martinez noticed a strong smell of grass and vanilla in the air that she'd somehow completely missed before.

Wilson caught her sniffing. "You'll also have a heightened sense of smell until the effect wears off. That only happens the first time. We don't know why."

She searched for the right words. "Smells like someone decided to drench themselves in vanilla extract and then mow the lawn."

"That'd be the books. You can barely notice it if you've got a sharp nose, but pumped up, it can be rather pungent."

As they approached the central reading desk, the shape of Chloe and Dot emerged exactly where Martinez had met them.

Both still had their heads down, intently reading, until Chloe caught their movement in her peripheral vision.

"How'd it go?" she burst. "Looks like it went well. It went well, didn't it?

"She's not raving, so yes, of course it went well," Dot answered her twin without looking up.

"Again, it's called being polite, Dot."

"Sure, that's what it's called."

"It went as good as can be expected," Wilson chimed in, quickly recognizing the signs of an impending fight; they didn't have time to get in the middle of one of Chloe and Dot's spats. "Agent Martinez was only out for a few minutes."

Martinez couldn't be sure, but it sounded like that was impressive. On a whim, she pried, "How long were you out, your first time."

Dot laughed. "He was down for an hour…thought we'd fried him."

"Do be nice, Dot," Chloe scolded. "Agent Wilson had a difficult acceptance period," she rephrased diplomatically. "Oh, I forgot! Here, have some water."

Martinez immediately accepted the bottle of water. As she poured it down her throat, it quenched a deep thirst she felt in her bones. Her condition immediately improved; her muscles relaxed and she rolled her shoulders back. "Thanks Chloe, that helped a lot." Chloe beamed as she threw the returned bottle into the recycling bin. "So, that…thing…down there, that demon—"

"Furfur's not a demon, he's a devil," Dot interrupted, "Devils make a deal with you and keep their end of it. Demons won't. They're straight up insane in the aetherial membrane."

"Fine. Then, that devil down there, he's under control, right?" It came out a little rawer than she had intended, but it wasn't every day you found out that devils were real and distinctly different than demons.

"Yes, he's harmless right now," Chloe assured her.

"Mostly harmless," Wilson corrected. "He can only reach past the pentagram with the smallest part of his powers, and as long as it's not broken—as long as nothing passes through the silver etching—he can't leave. He's trapped."

Martinez nodded and then had a thought. "Wait, how'd you get the stuff in there, then? That's a new game and the latest system."

"Beyond the couch is a much smaller circle we force him into when we want to move things about. He goes in because he wants entertainment and we—and by 'we,' I mean Leader—can release him from the smaller circle with just a command."

"So only Leader has control of him?"

"There's a reason she's the boss. She captured him back in the early 1990s, and he's one of the main reasons why we've been so successful in our mission."

"We prevent the spread of magic," Dot expounded. "Magic, all magic, is just shit. It always comes at a price, and the price is always greater than its benefit."

"Crudely put, but truthful," Chloe agreed with her sister. "But more than that, we prevent the use of magic by the enemies of our national interests."

"You're supernatural *spies*?" Martinez asked, finding the words coming out of her mouth patently ridiculous. Yet, after what she'd just experienced....

"More like supernatural detectives, with a bit of occasional spying on the side," Dot corrected. "And we're not, he is," she pointed at Wilson. "As you will be, if you accept the offer."

Martinez watched the three expectant faces scrutinizing her every muscle. "I don't really have a choice, do I?"

Wilson was about to respond, but Chloe preempted him; empathy wasn't his strong suit. "Not really, no," she answered as kindly she could. "You can decline, but the process of ensuring you don't betray us—purposefully or on accident—is rather unpleasant."

"Not everyone makes it out intact," Dot added bluntly. "Sometimes things can change."

The room went silent, waiting on Martinez, but she was still staring at the striated salt floor.

"Look, I understand that you'll need time," Wilson broke the uncomfortable silence after a time.

"No need. I'm in," she finally voiced. "If there are more of those things out there, more things like Furfur, they've got to be stopped. Someone inside the Salt Mine obviously did their homework and knew how appealing this job would be to me. And I'm sure I've been vetted twice to Sunday, so it would rude to say no and waste all their efforts."

"That'd be me," Dot affirmed with the first real smile Martinez had seen on her since they'd met. "And it would be four times to Sunday."

"We'd expect nothing less," Wilson complimented her with an appreciative nod. He found it best to praise her when she was in a good mood. Dot was, by far, the more difficult of the twins.

The mood had relaxed with Martinez's acceptance, but she'd started to feel woozy. A sudden wave of nausea hit her as Wilson was going over the agenda for the rest of the day. She grabbed ahold of the counter's edge to steady herself and tried to regain her equilibrium. Between pursed lips, she asked, "Could I get another bottle of water, Chloe? I think I'm not quite as fine as I thoug…" She burbled off before collapsing sideways into Wilson, who managed to catch her before she hit the floor for the second time this morning.

"Huh. Never seen that reaction before," Dot said, curiously peering over the desk.

Chapter Six

Aylesbury, Buckinghamshire, UK
8th of December, 6:55 p.m. (GMT)

DCI Jones's phone rang right as he was about to dive into the steaming steak and kidney pie the waitress at his favorite pub, the Heavy Plow, had just delivered to his table. He used to eat them more often, but on doctor's orders, he had cut back to once a week. He was annoyed at this disruption to his weekly indulgence until he checked the name of the caller: Dr. Andrew Brinston. Brinston was the medical examiner at Slough, where they'd sent the body of the deceased Mr. Carlmon Grollo.

He silently apologized to his pie and picked up the line. "Ah, Dr. Brinston, so glad to hear from you," he answered with honest appreciation; it was rare to get any results so quickly.

"Yes, yes, I'm sure it is," Brinston remarked off-hand; his voice had that permanently distracted tone common to many great intellectuals, of which Brinston was one. He could have had his pick of jobs in London or on the Continent, for that matter, but he preferred the small village life and owned several hectares adjacent to the Burnham Beeches Nature Preserve. If

Jones was remembering correctly, he had a couple of horses; he was one of those people. "Hate to bother you during dinner hour, but this case has proven simply extraordinary and I must request you come and see for yourself."

Jones leaned back against the solid old wooden chair—that was unexpected. "Certainly, Dr. Brinston. I could be there in, say, an hour? Traffic and weather considering."

"Sounds excellent! Hunt me down in the basement when you get here. I'll have everything completed and ready to go. Brinston out."

Jones would have said his goodbyes, but the doctor had already disconnected. He put the phone away, pondering what could work up the ME to such an extent. He'd find out soon enough, and his hour arrival time provided a solid twenty minutes for his pie. He tucked in and found himself ordering a pint of bitter before he was halfway through. It just seemed unfair to the pie not to.

Fortified with food and drink, DCI Jones made the drive from Aylesbury to Slough in good time, thanks to a bit of light speeding and the general lack of traffic this late on a cool December's night. His end destination was Slough Hospital, a concrete pile erected in the 1960s. As he left the warmth of his car, the buzzing florescent lights of the parking lot greeted him along with the mild hum of traffic. It was music to his ears.

He'd always loved the night, especially the urban night, but his wife would have none of it. "It's too risky! You have a family to think of now!" So he found himself bundled off to rural lands in his early twenties beside the woman he loved more than he probably should, and three bouncy bundles of endless energy. He didn't regret it, but he wouldn't say he didn't miss the city.

He entered the gray monolith and made his way to the morgue, flashing his badge at the lone measure of security the hospital employed to keep the general public out of the employees-only area. Before opening the door, he steadied himself: morgues could get to him and part of being a proper DCI meant not blanching at the sight of a human brain being weighed. After a moment of preparation, the door gave way under his hand and two bright full-spectrum lights accosted his eyes.

"Ah, DCI Jones, just on time, I see," Dr. Brinston remarked with a glance at the large digital clock on the wall. He was leaning over the body of the late Mr. Grollo, putting the penultimate closing stitches into the Y-shaped incision he'd made to open the body. Jones gave an internal sigh of relief as the truly gruesome stuff was finished; he could deal with parts in a jar because they weren't that different than the hundreds of other dead things in a jar he'd seen growing up with a biologist grandfather. "One more minute and I'll be done; please bear with me."

Jones waited quietly until the doctor made his final knot and the corpse was sealed again. Brinston removed his gloves to shake Jones's hand with gusto. "This one's for the scrap book, I tell you. Come look at this." He pointed at the body's face. "See the slight marking there on his neck? The little red dots?" Jones looked and nodded—they were very faint, and probably only visible under the bright full lights of the morgue.

"Those look like petechial hemorrhaging," Jones ventured.

"Well eyed, DCI," the ME complimented him. Jones had worked with him enough to understand the doctor's methods. Unlike others who would immediately tell you their findings, he liked to walk through the process with "his investigators," as he called the detectives of the Criminal Investigation Department. Ever the consummate student in a wide array of interests, Brinston had an unwavering faith in education and never failed to take advantage of a teaching moment in his field of specialty when it presented itself. Jones didn't mind the dance the doctor wanted and always allowed him the time he desired, if for no other reason than winning goodwill in case there was ever a need to call in a favor.

"But only on the neck? That's strange, isn't it? Normally they're on the eyes and face first before the neck, right?"

"Right again! It is rare to find them only on the neck, but it does happen, as you can see."

"So, asphyxiation then? I don't see any bruising around the neck, so that probably rules out strangulation."

"That's my finding," the doctor agreed. "And yes, there's no bruising, post-mortem or otherwise. The hyoid bone is also intact, although that in itself proves nothing."

A puzzled look crossed Jones's face. "Did he have a stroke or a heart attack?" He'd worked on a case once where the victim had stroked out face down in a pile of sand he was spreading across the bricks of his backyard. The stroke hadn't been enough to kill him, but he couldn't rouse himself, and a few minutes breathing in sand was all it took to end his life. Much more common were drownings caused by strokes or heart attacks, but you never forgot the weird ones encountered on the job.

"None that I detected," Brinston replied.

A cold wave washed over Jones. "So it's murder, then."

"I wouldn't jump to that particular conclusion yet, DCI Jones," the ME cautiously stated, waving Jones over to the far table of the morgue upon which sat a pile of partially assembled pieces and strips of painted fabric. "I found this in the victim's stomach."

Jones regarded the mass of multicolored fabric and put two and two together. "He was force-fed his paintings?" His stomach roiled at the image—what a horrific way to die. "That would have to be organized crime, then. That's one hell of a message to send to someone."

"Again with the jumping to conclusions," the ME chided.

Jones sighed and tried his best to not look irritated, but failed. "It's late, Doc; just tell me what you know."

"There wasn't any sign of struggle, so I'm putting forth the idea that he did it to himself."

"Pardon?"

"I know it sounds strange, but hear me out. See this group of small pieces here? I found these packed along the pyloric sphincter." The blank expression on the DCI's face prompted further explanation. "The 'end' of the stomach where it connects with the small intestines. The larger pieces were, for lack of a better term, atop the smaller ones, and then the long strips were at the peak of the stomach. What caused the asphyxiation was this thick long piece here—it lodged in his throat and cut off his oxygen supply."

"So he choked to death? There should be at least some petechial hemorrhaging in the eyes then, no?"

"Normally, yes. I don't have a working theory on that yet, other than not everything that one would expect always occurs. There was significant abrasion to the epiglottis consistent with the theory, however, so I'm willing to believe it's just an oddity."

"But all of that doesn't mean he wasn't forced—say, at gunpoint—to do this to himself."

"If that was the case, wouldn't he have continued to cut the paintings up into small pieces? I mean, would you voluntarily try to swallow this"—he again pointed at the killing strip—"when you obviously had the ability to make the pieces smaller like the first ones?"

"He could have been forced to eat larger and larger pieces," Jones persisted with his theory. "Didn't the ancient Mongols sometimes execute people by making them swallow progressively larger stones until they choked?"

"I'm not versed in the habits of the Mongols, DCI Jones," Brinston answered without a trace of sarcasm.

"And if he was doing it of his own volition, why did he increase the size of the pieces he was cutting?"

"I can't answer that, either. I'm still waiting on all his medical records. Perhaps he'd done something like this before. It's called pica: the desire and practice of eating non-nutritive materials. Develops temporarily in some women during pregnancy, but some people suffer from it chronically. There was one woman who methodically ate her entire couch and couldn't leave the house without taking some with her, in case she was detained for too long."

"You think maybe he had a mental disorder and it just got out of hand?" Jones wasn't pleased at how many "maybes" and "theories" were being thrown around, but that wasn't unusual in the beginning of an investigation. The facts would eventually unravel the mysteries.

"We won't know until I get all the records, but even then, he could have had it and simply never told anyone. You may want to inquire about it from the people closest to him. All I can really say is that the late Mr. Grollo wasn't forced, and by that, I mean actually physically forced to do this. He did it of his own will. It's up to you to figure out if it was his own 'free' will…that I cannot state with any certainty."

Jones nodded and thanked the ME for staying on late

before climbing back into his car and pointing the front end northward toward home, but not before sending his wife a text message that he was on his way. She worried when he was out at night, even when there wasn't cause, so he always let her know that things were fine.

But in the dark, alone with his thoughts, he wasn't sure things were fine. In fact, he had the unsettling feeling that things were most definitely not fine. He found himself checking the sides of the road on the way home, as if at any moment, something was going to rush out of the forest into the beaming headlights of his car.

Chapter Seven

Detroit, Michigan, USA
9th of December, 4:49 a.m. (GMT-5)

Martinez woke on a couch in a dark office. The first thing she did was pat her side. She breathed a little easier when she felt her gun in its holster and saw her bag on the floor beside her. She was still dressed in the clothes from her job interview, although they were quite rumpled and a little stale.

Judging from the walls and floor, she was still somewhere in the Salt Mine and someone had covered her in a drab, musty woolen blanket, something that could have been surplus from the last World War. A nearby digital clock illuminated the room, revealing a steel and wood desk set and the empty bookshelf behind. She reached into her leather bag and found her phone—no signal, but at least she knew what day it was and could confirm the time. She'd been out for almost twenty hours.

She kept the warm blanket around her as she rose, and her stomach growled when the bottle of water and cling-wrapped sandwich came into view on the top of the broad desk. She inhaled the first half of the ham and cheese sandwich and washed it down with half the bottle. A few rapid bites later, she finished its companion.

Once her stomach had something to chew on, she started replaying the events of yesterday, at least that which she remembered. Part of her mind wanted to forget, but she pushed past it, forcing herself to confront reality head on. Devils were real. Magic was real. Pentagrams weren't just for metal album covers.

And then, the memory of Furfur's change returned, like a hagfish clinging onto a dead whale. A wave of feelings crashed down on her, and she fought to keep her footing. Martinez wasn't the fainting type and she would be damned if it happened again. She went to a different part of her brain, one that analyzed things, and slowly processed all those emotions. As she turned down the faucet, the tsunami became a trickle.

Yes, it was horrific to watch, but she'd seen worse in movies, read worse in books, and definitely seen much worse in real life. She bit on her lip, trying to pin down *precisely* why it was so disturbing. To name a thing was to take away its power, especially things that relied on being unseen and unexamined. That's was one of the few things the mandated therapist had said that actually made sense to her—shine a light on the shadows.

No, the creepy part wasn't the thing itself; it was that it *didn't* seem out of place. Despite how absolutely wrong it felt, it was also completely normal. There were real monsters lurking out there; there was nothing allegorical or metaphorical about what she saw. And just as her conscious mind caught up with her gut, an idea bubbled up to the surface—if there was real evil, that meant there could also be real good. Lord knows, the world could use some real good.

Sound once more of body and mind, Martinez tossed the blanket on the couch and opened the door. The hallway was completely silent; there wasn't even a low rumble of a forced air system. She popped her head out, looking left and right. With no one in sight, she thought it was time to investigate. The Salt Mine probably knew everything about her, and what's good for the goose was good for the gander.

Upon examination, her own door had a palm scanner on the outside, but there was no way to be sure if it was working without risking getting locked out. She quietly picked up the chair and propped the door open. Then she fished out a small flashlight from her bag; the hall was bathed in low-light with only a fraction of the lights on. Before exiting, she shined her beam on the engraved brass plaque on the open door: Doppler.

She carefully stepped out of the office; to the left, a long hallway lined with doors, and to the right, a short passage to another room. The smooth salt floor made no sound against her soft soles as she veered left. Every thirty feet, a metal door bearing a nameplate punctured the crystalline walls, staggered to prevent offices opening directly opposite each other. Each was framed in metal with a palm scanner, and Martinez noted that most of them had a small buildup of dust on the handles. She mentally marked the names and doors with used handles as she reached the end of the hallway and turned around.

To the right was the common room, equally impressive as the fourth floor's. Martinez spied Agent Wilson asleep on one of the couches, covered by a blanket that matched the one that had been draped over her. He looked less serious in his sleep, with his crooked sleeping mask exposing his right eye to the dimmed lightening. The steady rise and fall of his chest indicated that it wasn't enough to wake him. She debated on rousing him but decided to take the opportunity to scout more.

She found a pair of restrooms at the back of the common room as well as a small kitchen. The refrigerator was nearly empty except for some bottled water; sadly, no more sandwiches. The hallway on the other side of the common room was much like the first: rows of doors with palmscanners and nameplates.

She helped herself to another bottle of water while she considered her options. All the offices that were occupied were locked, and all the ones that were open were either empty or otherwise uninteresting. Martinez macabrely wondered which of the offices in disuse belonged to the agents recently killed on the job.

Martinez shivered and rubbed her hands over the goosebumps under her clothes. It was a constant 55° F this deep in the earth, and while technically warmer than the outside, it was far from cozy. She headed back to the office of former Agent Doppler, which she'd initially thought an odd name until she had seen that all of them were like that. She put the chair back in its place and retrieved the rest of her things as well as the olive blanket—it may be ratty, but it was warm. Cloaked in wool, she used her hand to gently shut the door and descended to the common room.

With nothing else to investigate on this floor and no way to make the elevator move, she eased into one of the fine leather chairs and pulled out her phone. She'd downloaded a novel for the flight from Oregon but never got around to opening it. Burrowed into her woolen cocoon, she settled into a good book, switching scrolling hands to give them time to warm up before their next stint on the screen. A distinct thud and rumble startled her when the heating finally kicked on an hour later. It also roused Wilson from his sleep on the couch opposite her chair. "Agent Martinez?" he mumbled groggily, one uncovered eye staring at her. "Feeling better?"

She closed her book. "Yeah. Thanks for the sandwich."

"No problem." He yawned, pulling off the mask and propping himself up on one arm, "What time is it?"

"A little after six," she informed him and put away her phone. He yawned and stretched like a bear coming out of hibernation, and she waited patiently for him to fully wake before asking questions. "Wanna tell me where we are and what happened?"

“We’re on the fifth floor of the Salt Mine, where the agents have offices,” he answered them in order. “And yesterday, you passed out while we were talking with Chloe and Dot. We had one of the doctors in to check on you. She said there wasn’t anything wrong, so we let you sleep it off.”

Martinez nodded. “So what’s the plan now?”

Wilson sat up and ran his hands through his short brown hair, smoothing down the points that formed while he slept. “I told Leader you accepted, so she’s supposed to have a program ready for us this morning around seven, so not much longer.”

He stood and shook out the blanket before finding the corners. “I keep two of these old bastards in my office—not very comfortable, but warm as hell. They’ll probably outlast me.” He adroitly folded it in half three times and tucked the tidy rectangle under one arm. “I need to grab some breakfast. Care to join me? The cafeteria here isn’t great, but it’s filling.”

“Filling sounds perfect,” she answered, shedding the blanket and mimicking Wilson’s folds. She followed him to his office and nonchalantly waited in the hall while he opened the door with his palm. She read the nameplate on the door as he deposited the blankets inside: Fulcrum. That gave her guide no less than three names.

He meticulously closed the door behind him, and they took the elevator to the first floor. It resembled the layout of the fifth floor, except there was no large common room; instead, the space was partitioned into semi-private workspaces. A few people were already at work, but most of the desks were empty. Some nodded at Wilson, but most ignored the pair as they made their way to the back. The aroma of fresh bread filled the small hallway that opened up into the cafeteria.

It was little more than a long rectangular room with tables and seating. On one end stood two refrigerated cases filled with a variety of premade sandwiches and drinks while a short hot-food buffet bar lined the other. Wilson made his way to the hot food and loaded up on eggs, bacon, and toast. Martinez joined him, and they grabbed a seat in a secluded corner after filling cups of coffee and juice from nearby machines.

"This isn't half bad," Martinez commented after the first few bites.

"I'm not sure how Leader does it, but the stuff here's fresh and decent." They ate in silence, shoveling warm food into their cold, empty stomachs.

"So, why the big display yesterday?" Martinez asked obliquely in case anyone was listening.

He shrugged. "It's the last part of the job interview—any potential agent jumps right into the deep end. Better to have first exposure take place in a safe, controlled environment than in the field."

"And you don't waste any time on someone who can't handle the aether," Martinez astutely surmised.

"There is that," he conceded. "But it's also a fast way to convince people it's real. I mean, would you have believed me, really believed me, without that level of proof?"

Martinez prided herself on being open-minded and wanted to say it was possible, but eventually she acquiesced. "No. No, I wouldn't have."

"I wouldn't have either. That demonstration isn't necessary when recruiting people who already know magic is real, but unfortunately, those people are often lacking in the other skills necessary for being a field agent."

"So Leader tries to find people with the right skill set that would also be able to handle the supernatural stuff," she filled in the blanks. Wilson tilted his head to affirm her statement. "How many agents are there, besides the two of us?"

He took another bite of egg, thinking. "I'd have to check the records to make sure, but at least seven, if I'm not missing anyone."

Martinez suspected he knew exactly how many agents there were and all their codenames, but she let it slide. She was finally getting some answers out of Wilson, even if they were imprecise and vague.

She found him both intentional and slippery. He never gave away more information than he must, and even the things that seemed trivial or benignly unimportant seemed deliberate, like his sleeping mask leaving one eye uncovered. Did it slip or was it set up that way?

There was an economy in his manner, and nearly everything he said or did—or failed to do—seemed precisely calculated. If she had to sum him up in a single word, it would be *dissembling*. What gave her pause was that she didn't know if his constant obfuscation was simply habit of good tradecraft or covering up something more concerning. Then again, what could be more concerning than a devil in your basement?

They finished breakfast, deposited their dishes at the intake counter, and proceeded to Wilson's office to kill a few minutes before their meeting with Leader. Once they were back in the secure elevator, Martinez felt comfortable enough to speak openly; she still didn't know how much the average Salt Mine employee knew about what they were doing.

"So, I'm going to be a supernatural agent..." she mulled the notion over while they walked.

"That's the intent," Wilson curtly replied.

"How, exactly, does one train for that?"

"Generally speaking, you should already have most of the mundane practical skills via your FBI background. There will be some extended coursework at the Farm," Wilson colloquially referred to Camp Peary in Virginia where the CIA often trained. He opened the door to his office and motioned for Martinez to enter before closing the door. "Then, there will be a few courses taught by Chloe and Dot. Barring any unusual circumstances, you should be ready for beginning operations in six to twelve months."

Martinez took a seat in the red chair opposite Wilson's desk. "Magic's real," she sighed. "I expect it will eventually make sense."

"Well, yes and no," Wilson hemmed. "No matter how much you acclimate yourself to it, it still doesn't really make complete sense."

"Neither did gravity before Newton or germs before the microscope," Martinez countered. "Or particle physics for the modern age."

Wilson leaned back in his leather chair and considered her supposition. "In emerging science, we lack the understanding of the reasons of why something happens, but the outcomes are replicable, even when the results are baffling and unexplained as of yet. That is not the case with magic; it's not 'science we don't understand.' It's irrational at its core nature."

"There has to be some constancy. Otherwise, how could you cage something like Furfur?" she argued. His momentary silence led her to believe she had made a valid point.

"What is replicable can be repeated in very constrained parameters. X artifact does X, reliably. Person Y performs a set of actions and can now do this, reliably. But if another item is made that is the same to X in all respects, it doesn't have to work. Or if some other person performs exactly the same actions as Y, it's possible that nothing happens. In a system that has rational underpinnings, that shouldn't occur. If gravity worked like magic does, apples might only fall down when they drop on Isaac Newton's head, but otherwise, they don't *have to* fall to the ground. But they can when it suits them."

Martinez churned on the analogy. "So how do you know what works and doesn't work?"

"That's part of what you'll learn with the twins," he answered. "But there is one small consistency throughout everything that we've encountered: magic is powered from unconscious association, things we have integrated so completely into our being that we cannot turn them off."

"Like reflexes?" Martinez hazarded a guess.

"That's not a bad comparison," he agreed. "If I punch at your face, you pull back and blink. If you're suddenly thrown into water, you automatically hold your breath. But that's not quite what I'm talking about. Reflexes are programmed ways of reacting to stimulus that can be overridden. If you really wanted to, you could choose to not flinch, choose to breathe in a lungful of water. What I'm referring to cannot both exist and not exist. Once acquired, it simply is."

Martinez's brow knitted and Wilson tried a different tactic, one that had been shown to him many years ago. He opened one of the drawers and pulled out a blank piece of paper and a pink highlighter. The tip squeaked as he wrote, and he used his other hand to conceal it from her view.

"All you have to do is not understand what I've written down. But you *do* have to look at it." He flipped the paper over and she immediately saw the words, "DO NOT READ ME."

"See? You can't do it," he remarked immediately, knowing she'd failed. "No matter how hard you try, if you're fluent in a written language, you cannot stop understanding it just because you want to. It's automatic and you can't turn it off once you've got it. You'll never, ever, be able to choose to *not* understand a language once you're fluent in it. That's the level of unconscious association that successful magicians have." He victoriously capped the highlighter.

"Something so integrated that it's inseparable from you and you can't elucidate how or why it makes sense to you, just that it does," Martinez took a stab.

"Precisely!" Wilson exclaimed. With a single sweep of the hand, he quickly ran the piece of paper through a triple-pass shredder before proceeding. "The language metaphor can be extended to include contextual *and* subtextual meaning. If you are fluent in English, you may understand the literal meaning of English words, but if you learned it in America and are speaking to someone who learned theirs in Australia, you could easily miss a lot of meaning that would be obvious to another Aussie. Even English speakers from the same place could miss on subtext that's dependent on education, culture, and exposure."

"So those movies showing people in masks and robes holding occult rituals and chanting in ancient tongues?" Martinez asked.

Wilson shook his head. "I've lost count of how many magicians or witches I've encountered claiming magical talent whose only ability was to see what they wanted to see."

"Are there words that have inherent power?" Martinez tested the boundaries of this whole new world.

"Sort of, but just saying them out loud usually isn't enough." Wilson searched for the right analogy. "Think of it like potential energy versus kinetic energy. Say some magician in the sixteenth century wrote a demonology book in Latin and included magically imbued words. It has the potential to have supernatural effects, but if someone isn't at least fluent in Latin, that potential is not going to turn into kinetic magical energy."

She shook her head grimly. "You're killing *Evil Dead* for me, Wilson."

"That was Sumerian, not Latin," he pointed out, "but same rules apply."

"Well, at least they got the primitive screwheads right," she said with resignation.

The olive box on Wilson's desk buzzed and blinked; he pressed and held the offending button. "This is Wilson and Martinez."

"Leader's not going to be able to make it today," a well-spoken tenor announced though the speaker. "Orders are for Agent Martinez to go to HR, get an onboarding packet and temporary identification, and report back tomorrow at nine a.m. You're to meet her as you did yesterday."

"Will do. Fulcrum out." He released the blinking button and severed the line. "I guess we'll have to wait until tomorrow for the full plan. Let me escort you to HR."

Chapter Eight

Cambridge, Massachusetts, USA
9th of December, 10:30 a.m. (GMT-5)

"And with that, ladies and gentlemen, I call this meeting to an end," Charles Winston Roberts concluded to the rows of faces down the long table before him. "Thank you for attending, and good day." The suits somberly gathered their belongings and trickled out of the boardroom; their usual friendly banter was absent—no inquiries into family life, future plans, or side business.

Only one person lingered: Martin Phillips, CFO of Detrop Pharmaceuticals. He rubbed the short flaming red stubble on his head and straightened his hopelessly out-of-fashion glasses with his pianist's hands, marred by an old chemical burn acquired in a misspent youth. "Well, that was a goddamn bombshell, Chuck," Phillips remarked gravely. "You've made several enemies today, and there's going to be hell to pay once the shareholders get wind of this. The lid's only going to stay on for a few hours…maybe a whole day, if you're lucky."

"I know, Martin, but I've made up my mind. We've

increased the bottom line by fifteen percent every year for the past five years—rough years for the industry, I might add—so I'm willing to take more of their heat," Roberts replied, running his hands through his unruly hair. "They won't like it. They'll bitch and moan and promise hellfire, and then they'll shut up and console themselves with all the money I'm still making them." Roberts hurled the last of his things into his attaché case.

And they say redheads have a fiery disposition, Phillips thought to himself. He was one of Roberts's oldest friends, and as CFO, he had talked him out of things before, but his gut told him this time was different. Still, he had to try. "You're really serious about this, aren't you?" he probed gently.

"Martin, you of all people know that Detrop Pharmaceuticals is going to be plenty profitable next year. We're only going to lose, what, four percent off of what we could have made next year by releasing the patent on these two medications. A lousy four percent."

"Yes, but that four percent ends up being about *forty percent* of our profit for the year," Phillips pointed out.

"Which still leaves us well in the black with the remaining sixty percent profit!" Roberts screamed. Philips physically leaned away from him, taken aback by the raw emotion behind the words. They'd had their share of whoppers over the years, but it was never personal. This felt personal.

As Philips was slowly realizing that he wasn't going to be

able to change Roberts's mind, Roberts stared out the thirty-second-floor window and an immense fatigue set in. He watched the small cars and figures scurrying downtown Boston over the Charles River and grew morose. *How many times do we have to have the same fight?*

The exhausted man felt like surrendering—not to Martin and his four percent—but to the darkness. The inevitable end. The big nothing. "You tell me, Martin, when it is enough?"

"What?"

"What percent is enough? When does all this"—he waved his hands around the lush executive boardroom—"end up being enough? What percent does it take before we're satisfied? Before we've eaten everything we wanted at the meal and decide to share what we can't finish with those not at the table?" His hollow, tired eyes bore into Phillips's with a desperate look. "Just how much do we have to eat before we're full?"

Phillips didn't know what Roberts wanted to hear, so he said nothing. He longed for the early days, when it was just him, Roberts, and Emily Thibodeaux scrambling to turn Blandon Generics into the powerhouse that was Detrop Pharmaceuticals. There were no shareholders or board of directors, just the three of them spending countless hours working the business. Finding a bank that would give them a loan, scraping up sufficient collateral, getting the first production batch out on time, making their first public offer—it was hell, but it was the kind of forge in which unbreakable bonds were formed.

They were younger then, too foolish to be daunted by the scale of their endeavor. There was a fire in Roberts's eyes when he'd talked about the future of the company like it was already real, like Chuck had peered through the veil of time and was already seeing it in a way that neither he nor Emily could. That was why they followed him; they knew he was either going to create something incredible or crash and burn in a blaze of glory, but either way, his conviction made you want to be in the room when it happened.

Phillips didn't see any trace of that now, and frankly, he was frightened for the man standing in front of him. Where the fire of an inevitable and prosperous future once burned, he saw ashes. No one wanted to join in whatever future he was seeing in those dark and weary eyes.

"What going on, Chuck?" Phillips pleaded. "There's something you're not telling me. What's wrong, man?"

A wave of indecision and ambivalence rippled across Roberts's face before it settled; Phillips could see his friend struggling. "Nothing, Martin. Just feeling old, I guess. And tired. Perhaps I should take a vacation?" he suggested with slumped shoulders and resignation. "I'm sure Emily could handle things for a few weeks. I'd always be in contact by e-mail and phone, of course."

Roberts turned around toward the window again, his back signaling the end of discussion. He thought the moment had passed, but he couldn't be sure—although his voice sounded normal, even he could see the emptiness in his eyes reflected back at him. He needed help. He was sick and needed his medicine.

*****

Martin Phillips tried to put the disturbing meeting behind him and spent the rest of the morning clearing out his inbox until lunch. He grabbed a quick bite from Loco Tacos—the *best* taco truck in town—and decided that if Roberts was going to stonewall him, he needed to find a battering ram. They'd known each other too long for him to let this lie, even if his friend seemed to indicate that's what he wanted. Phillips spent the next several hours diving into the finances of Detrop Pharmaceuticals, in particular the activities of its CEO, but found nothing unusual.

This somewhat soothed his worry. Roberts was a smart guy, but financially, he wasn't much above an educated layman—if he had been doing anything questionable, the checks Phillips performed should've caught them. Financial business shenanigans ruled out, Phillips spitballed a litany of other potential problem areas: relationships, drugs, gambling, and kinky shit people prefer to keep secret.

As far as he knew, Roberts wasn't currently in a relationship. His whatever-it-was with David had ended a little more than a year ago, and he hadn't seen anyone seriously since. Since he was single again, the kinky possibility couldn't be ruled out, but Roberts had never been shy about his sex life or his peccadillos. Phillips was hard pressed to think that there was something he'd been hiding for so long that neither Thibodeaux nor himself knew about; since college, they'd never failed to share their personal preferences openly, Thibodeaux being such a nurturing—and nosy—creature.

There was always the chance of something new developing, but Roberts looked haunted, not shy or embarrassed. And from Phillips's understanding, discovering a love of S&M usually makes people feel *better*, not worse. He felt that he couldn't rule it out, but it seemed awfully unlikely.

It could be drugs—that would account for the mood swings and recent changes in personality, if only it wasn't contrary to decades of history. Roberts had always been straight-edged, as they'd called it back then. He'd caught a lot of flak about it, including from Thibodeaux and Phillips, but he never budged on his stance. However, being a CEO of a pharmaceutical company would pretty much provide unlimited access to whatever substances were desired, and if Roberts was using, he wouldn't be the first executive to dip into his own supply. Phillips put everything on hold and dove into the records again, this time checking on the meds themselves—inventories and activities of samples, shipping discrepancies, and quality control histories—but as with the financials, everything came up normal.

By the time five o'clock rolled around, Phillips knew nothing more than what he'd known at lunch. The only thing left on his list was gambling, but without access to Roberts's private financial statements, it was going to be much harder to look into. There was little he could do from here except check on Roberts's business trips, and sure enough, he'd taken several trips to Vegas in the past six months. Unfortunately, Vegas was the hub of business conferences and his last visit was a pharmaceutical conference three months ago—hardly the actions of a gambling addict.

Phillips tapped his finger against his chin and told his now-hungry stomach to shut up. Looking out the window of his corner office at a beautiful sunset, he was befuddled. There wasn't anything else he could think of. He donned his heavy winter coat and elected for a fresh pair of eyes—he'd run it by Thibodeaux and see what she thought. *If anyone can get Chuck to talk, it will be Emily.*

*****

The cold rain made parking difficult; it seemed like the entire neighborhood had decided to stay in for the evening. After several circles, Emily Thibodeaux found a spot for her Tesla Model S, and she and Martin Phillips made the mad dash down half a block to Roberts's front door. Huddled under an umbrella designed for one, they rang the doorbell, exhaling clouds of vapor like mini steam engines.

"I hope he's home," Phillips voiced concern. "I didn't see his car."

"That doesn't mean anything—you saw the street. Maybe he had to park faraway too. Look, there's a light on the third floor," Thibodeaux pointed out, holding her hands to her mouth and warming them as Phillips held the umbrella. "He's got to be home; you know how Chuck hates to waste energy."

"Well, he's taking his sweet time," he groused as drops of frigid water dripped off the too-small umbrella, down his jacket, and onto his pant leg.

"He's got a lot of stairs. Give him time," she said casually. "We're not as young as we used to be."

"No, we're not, but he looks like he aged twenty years overnight," he warned her. She'd been out of town the past three weeks dealing the overseas manufacturing issues and import opportunities. She hadn't seen Roberts in almost a month.

Thibodeaux squeezed his flexed arm that held the umbrella. "We'll get to the bottom of it."

The polished wooden door creaked open and a wan and pale face emerged. "Can I help you?" Roberts croaked, not even recognizing his closest friends.

"Chuck? It's us," Thibodeaux spoke tentatively, shocked at the specter of her friend that answered the door. He'd looked perfectly healthy before she'd left for China.

"Jesus, Chuck! You look like hell warmed over!" Phillips

exclaimed. Concern overriding decorum, he handed the umbrella to Thibodeaux and pushed himself into the house. He put a firm hand on Roberts, who wearing shorts and a t-shirt and was cold to the touch. "Let's get you upstairs and under some blankets."

Roberts wanted to deny that he needed their help, but couldn't find any energy to argue. He let himself be led up to the second-story living room, onto a Nella Vetrina Babylon leather sofa, and under a massive king-sized comforter Thibodeaux grabbed from the third-floor linen closet. "Hey guys," Roberts mumbled with a soft, dopey smile once he was fully ensconced in his newly made nest. His eyes had a faraway glaze and his words slurred slightly.

"Does he have a fever?" Thibodeaux asked Phillips.

"His forehead feels normal," Phillips responded after checking with the back of his hand. "Where do you keep your thermometer, Chuck?"

"Master bedroom, medicine cabinet," he answered dreamily before closing his eyes and burrowing into his blanket. Thibodeaux nodded and headed upstairs. After she left, Phillips quietly pressed, "What's happening, man? Something's definitely going on. You wanted to tell me after the meeting, but you shut me out instead. What's eating you?"

Roberts didn't respond. In fact, Roberts didn't even hear him. He felt like he was floating on a warm fuzzy cloud and everything was receding. For the first time in a long time, he didn't feel bad.

"Emily! Hurry up with that thermometer!" Phillips yelled, hoping he could be heard up so many flights of stairs. He shook Roberts but didn't get a response, and dialed 911. He wasn't sure how to phrase what was going on, and he went with "non-responsive but breathing" when questioned, citing that Roberts hadn't looked very good earlier in the day.

Thibodeaux heard the end of the conversation from a floor up and bounded down the final flight of stairs. "Is he okay?"

"He's not responding when I shake him." Phillips demonstrated. Roberts just flopped about, a goofy grin on his face that terrified both of them.

"Check his arms, check his arms!" she hurriedly ordered. "Track marks?" Thibodeaux hated to think of it, but she'd lost her brother to heroin when she was a freshmen in high school.

"Oh hell, you don't think?" Phillips voiced his doubt but did as he was told. He pulled the comforter the rest of the way off. Phillips ran his fingers and eyes down both arms. "Clean! Nothing here," he reported triumphantly.

Thibodeaux was not satisfied. "I'm going to check his toes. If he's been hiding it…" But his feet were free of unusual marks. Both breathed a sigh of relief that they couldn't see any signs of intravenous drug use.

They searched on their phone for what to do while they waited for the ambulance to arrive. After ensuring he was still breathing fine, they rolled him onto his side and covered him the comforter just to be safe. As they adjusted the blanket, a golden coin dropped from Roberts's pocket with a solid thunk on the wide-plank pine floor.

Thibodeaux was closest and picked it up, puzzled. "What's this?" she asked, handing it to Phillips, who had an extensive coin collection, including three copper 1943 pennies that he was inordinately proud of.

"It's a new Maple Leaf, a Canadian gold coin," he added when the name drew a blank on Thibodeaux's face. He rolled the coin in his hand. "But look here. It looks like it's been bitten into." He rubbed his fingers over the ridges.

"Bitten? Is that a coin collector thing?"

"No, Emily. We're not prospectors in the old west; there are better ways to tell if it's real gold now," he sardonically replied. But her comment gave him an idea. Thibodeaux instantly recognized the look on his face—he had a notion that he didn't like, but it fit the working parameters. He gently pried open Roberts's mouth.

"What is it?" she demanded after a few seconds.

"It doesn't make any sense," he muttered incredulously.

"What doesn't make sense, Martin?"

The redhead looked up. "Chuck's never had dental work, right?"

"No, remember how smug he was about it when I had to get a root canal last year?"

Phillips moved so Thibodeaux could see into their old

friend's mouth. The crowns of his molars were golden and smooth, like he'd eaten a mouthful of taffy that was stuck to his teeth and smothering their contours. Thibodeaux gaped in horror and disbelief.

"Christ, Martin…he's been *eating* gold?" Thibodeaux whispered as the blaring sirens approached the house.

Chapter Nine

Detroit, Michigan, USA
28th of December, 6:00 a.m. (GMT-5)

The sounds of tropical island rain gently brought Martinez out of her sleep. She kept her eyes closed and lolled around in bed for a few minutes, pretending she was somewhere warm and sunny instead of Detroit in winter. She turned off the recording she'd used as an alarm and the bird calls abruptly ended. *Time to get up*, she gave herself a pep talk before flipping the covers off. All the warmth left the bed and she started her day.

She got the small twenty-four-ounce hotel coffee pot going before getting ready. It was going to be another day of cramming with Chloe and Dot—she had done little else since accepting the position nearly three weeks ago. There was no dress code at the Salt Mine, but she stuck with business attire. After years with the bureau, it had become her professional armor, and she would have felt naked without it.

Coffee in hand and humming a tune, she descended the stairs and grabbed a croissant from the complimentary continental breakfast bar for later. Normally, she had no problems eating and driving, but she paid closer attention navigating the wintry roads of Detroit. Although an excellent driver on dry and wet roads, she'd never had much experience on snow and ice, and she was feeling her way into it.

She'd tried to trade her rear-wheel drive model for an AWD Charger at the rental agency after a few slips during acceleration, but it had been a bust. With some sadness, she gave up the muscle car and accepted one of the two Subarus they'd had in their fleet. She could use all the help she could get navigating the treacherous road conditions before she fishtailed into some trouble.

When she wasn't busy studying for her new job—which turned out to be the best-paying job she'd probably ever get, since all Salt Mine workers got paid standard rates from both the FBI and the CIA—she was looking for permanent housing and vacillating between renting and buying. The Detroit housing market was vastly more affordable than the Pacific Northwest, and there were some rather amazing old houses that just needed a little TLC for the price of a one-bedroom apartment in Portland. Looking in winter was also a boon, as all the listings that didn't sell last summer tended to drop in price.

However, buying would require selling her place in Oregon first. It wouldn't be hard to find a buyer, but there was a finality to it. It would sever the last tie she had to her old life, and she was only three weeks into the new one. So it was hotel living for the time being.

She followed the Zug Island exit to the guard station and wrestled the badge from her bag. "Heya Georgie! How're the kids?" she warmly inquired, handing over her cover ID: Tessa Marvel, Assistant Director of Acquisitions. The Monday guard's wife had just had twins ten days ago.

"They're doing great! But I tell ya, it's amazing how little sleep we're getting when they seem to spend most of *their* time asleep. They weren't kidding when they say twins are double trouble," he gabbed with a rueful but contented smile. "If you catch me taking a nap, don't tell anyone!" he joked.

"You can rely on my discretion," she replied with a conspiratorial grin before he waved her through. She parked, grabbed her coffee, and suddenly realizing she hadn't yet eaten her croissant. She stuffed the flaky pastry in her mouth as she hustled out of her parked car. It wasn't like she had to punch in at a time clock at this job, but she hated being late. Unless there was an act of God, she considered tardiness a sign of poor planning or plain inconsiderateness.

The elevator doors opened and Abrams's chipper mechanical voice greeted her, "Good Morning, Martinez!" Martinez mumbled something approaching "good morning" through her breakfast and dropped off her stuff in the slot on the left wall. Once she'd finished her bite, she made small talk with Abrams, asking how her weekend was. Abrams was an endless reservoir of mindless sociable chatter, and Martinez had learned to open the conversation and let her fill the time as the machine scanned her possessions. It was simply a matter of nodded and adding a "you don't say?" every now and then, and everyone left the encounter happy.

Now that Martinez was in the system, she summoned the elevator with her own palm. She knew it was stupid to be excited about such a trivial thing, but she liked the independence it gave her. She didn't have to rely on having a guide or babysitter to get to her office anymore.

The common room of the fifth floor was empty as usual. Martinez found it a little creepy her first few days—so much space with so little life—but came to appreciate the silence. Sometimes, she'd bring her reading to the common room for a change of scenery from her office. The kind-hearted would euphemistically call the decor "mid-century," but Martinez personally thought of it as "Cold War chic."

Every piece of furniture in her office was from the 1950s or '60s, and none of them matched each other. It hadn't been used in decades and the last agent who'd occupied the space, codename Patron, hadn't redecorated during his tenure. In all honesty, Martinez wouldn't have been surprised if the agent prior to him hadn't changed anything either. But it was adjacent to Wilson's office, and the new nameplate had already been installed. She was officially codename Lancer.

Besides her and Wilson, there were five other agents. She'd only met two of them, Aurora and Prism. Clover, Deacon, and

Hobgoblin were out on long cases and hadn't returned to the Mine since she'd arrived. According to Wilson, such long cases weren't unusual; his longest had been more than five months. The agents were polite to each other but far from cordial; Martinez wasn't surprised that there was no holiday office party or Secret Santa exchange among this lot.

Be it ever so humble, she sung to herself as she opened the door with her palm and flicked the light switch on the wall. The fluorescent lights flickered before fully engaging, casting a pale yellow cast over her outdated workspace. She put down her coffee, hung her coat on the chrome coat rack affixed to the wall, and flicked on the table lamp before turning off the overhead lights. The softer light made the place less austere and she preferred it for reading.

A dozen old books were piled on the corner of the giant table, and Martinez checked the day's reading list to find out which one she should dive into first. Today's subject was colonial magic—the imposition and intersection of Western magical theology and spiritualism upon the world's indigenous populations. The associated reading was from *The Real History of Magic* written by Chloe and Dot in conjunction with references to passages from the stack of primary source books on her desk.

She'd never had much interest in magic or the occult—which she now knew to be different things—and she would have been lost without the twins' organizational work. Without their careful grooming of the material, Martinez would have little hope of determining the sliver of truth from the ramblings. All of the texts were in such flowery and obtuse language, they were nearly unintelligible even when they were imparting truth about "the arts." According to Dot, ninety-nine percent of the stuff that was written down was complete bunk. The thought of trying to do this on her own made her shudder.

She was an hour into her studies when a knock fell on her door. She quizzically tilted her head—she wasn't expecting anyone. She stretched as she rose and opened the door to Wilson. "Leader's got a mission for us," he tersely informed her.

Well, good morning to you, too, she thought to herself before voicing an inquisitive, "Us?"

"That's what she said," he said.

"But I'm still in training. And I thought we worked alone?" she objected in her confusion.

"You are correct on both counts, but when Leader beckons, we come," he laid it out plainly. "We're supposed to meet her in her office at nine."

She nodded and waved at the pile of research on her desk. "Will you grab me when the time comes? I sometimes get lost in this."

"Will do." He checked his watch and recalculated his morning. "I'll come back in forty-five minutes."

Left to her reading, she tried to refocus, but the excitement of her first real mission was too distracting. She picked up one of Chloe and Dot's other works, *The Exhaustive Symbolic Dictionary*, and paged through the thousands of compiled symbols while she mentally counted down the minutes.

Chapter Ten

Detroit, Michigan, USA
28th of December, 8:55 a.m. (GMT-5)

Leader's office was on the fourth floor, the lowest level accessible to Salt Mine employees with a low security clearance. When Wilson and Martinez arrived with five minutes to spare, they were greet by David LaSalle, Leader's private secretary-slash-bodyguard. He was a brick of a man over six feet tall, and his suit did little to hide his broad shoulders and muscular physique. He was always polite and professional to Martinez, but she wouldn't want to be on the wrong side of Leader's assistant. She doubted his secretarial skills got him the job, even though he could type eighty words per minute, kept impeccable records, and had a way of arranging the impossible at the last minute.

When the appointed time came, LaSalle ushered them into Leader's office. Cut out from the salt, it was twice the size of the agents' offices and furnished in a no-nonsense manner. Function was the winning concern, followed by comfort, with aesthetics limping across the finishing line after those two had long ago packed up and gone home—that was how Leader liked it. The only hint of artistic indulgence was the single painting that adorned the walls, a high-quality reproduction of *The Temptation of Saint Anthony* by Jan Brueghel the Elder.

The back wall was lined with filing cabinets with an imposing desk in front of them. Its patina and well-worn edges and corners attested to years of use. Martinez thought such a petite person would be diminished behind such a large piece of furniture, but Leader's presence filled the space from which she ruled the roost.

"Fulcrum and Lancer for your nine o'clock, ma'am," LaSalle announced, using their codenames.

"Thank you, David," she acknowledged. She motioned to the agents. "Please have a seat." The white leather chairs in front of her desk were oversized, and Martinez felt like Lily Tomlin's little girl in a big chair when she took the chair next to Wilson. LaSalle closed the door behind him and they waited as Leader put away the file in her hand and pulled another from a different cabinet.

Martinez observed her elusive boss intently while her back was to them. It was easier to think when she wasn't staring at you with those hawkish gray eyes. She'd seen Leader a couple of times during the past few weeks, but most of her contact during onboarding was with Wilson, Chloe and Dot, and for administrative things, LaSalle.

Leader dressed according to the same principles as her office's decor; today it was a cabled russet sweater over khakis.

On the rare occasions where presentation was of primary importance, she wore a suit masterfully and played the part, but she never put too much stock in appearances. Things were rarely what they seemed, and all that glitters is not gold.

Leader deposited the new files on her desk and took a seat in her executive chair. Without bothering to engage in niceties, she queried Wilson from her perch. "How's Lancer's training going?"

"It's going well, according to Dot and Chloe, but she's still a long way from mission-ready," Wilson replied. A small part of Martinez felt slighted, but she wholeheartedly agreed with his assessment. The amount of information she was required to know was daunting, to say the least.

"It would be unrealistic to think she would be at this juncture," Leader stated matter-of-factly, "which is why I'm sending you on a mission together. I want to start including field operations during the training period." She didn't give either of them time to object and proceeded with the briefing.

"Over the past two months, there've been a series of five suspicious deaths: North Carolina, India, Spain, Ireland, and most recently, England. There are murmurings in Interpol of an organized crime effort or possibly terrorism with some unknown goal. They're far from sure that anything's happening, but the death of five pharmaceutical CEOs has their attention. They haven't formally started an investigation, which is where you two come in.

"The first death occurred in Durham, North Carolina. The CEO of Tigris Pharmaceuticals was found dead from a heroin overdose. The second was in Ayodhya, India—drowned and found floating in the Ganges. The third, in Barcelona, Spain, died from a car wreck due to illegal street racing. The worst was in Dublin, Ireland—the CEO was killed by a prostitute who claimed that he'd tried to eat her. The investigation found two partially eaten female corpses rotting in his house, adding credibility to her story. She was subsequently cleared of wrongdoing."

"I'd heard of that one," Wilson chimed in. "Particularly gruesome." Martinez kept quiet; she suspected she hadn't gained speaking privileges yet.

Leader nodded and continued, "The most recent occurred about three weeks ago. The CEO died from asphyxiation—apparently he choked to death while eating the paintings in his drawing room."

"Different countries, different methods, and nothing that connects them except their jobs?" Wilson mulled aloud. "Could be the work of an excellent mechanic, although I'm at a loss at what could be used to drive a person to cannibalism."

"That's the one that raised my suspicions and the fact that it was followed by death-from-fine-art has swayed me to assign it to you. It's possible that they're not related, but two strange deaths in a row warrants investigation. David has your packets ready. You're booked for the 11:35 to London. Lancer, you'll need to go to HR to be issued a company card, and you'll need to borrow one of Fulcrum's suitcases."

*****

Once he was back in his office, Wilson allowed himself a moment of frustration. It was one thing to be the contact point for a brand new agent, but another to do a mission with one. Working in tandem with an experienced operative would have been annoying but tolerable, but sending him out into the field with a newbie that had barely finished onboarding meant he had to do all the work, spend time educating Martinez, and make sure she didn't do anything stupid. Not that it was her fault—it would be unfair to expect her not to make mistakes at this point in her training. She might have been an ace FBI agent, but there was no way for her to know the wide potential of supernatural dangers out there. Not yet.

He groused a little more before pulling himself together; Martinez was getting her card, complete with a fake history of expenses, and she would arrive at any moment. *In all matters, before beginning, a diligent preparation should be made*, he calmed himself, quoting Cicero. *That's all the anger time you get.*

Wilson resigned himself to be ever vigilant and to constantly remind himself what a complete novice didn't know to get them safely through this assignment. It would be a difficult mind-space to conduct an operation, but he didn't really have a choice. That's the way it was, and the alternative could get them both killed.

He took out his three pre-packed suitcases and unloaded Cold and Temperate onto his desk, mingling them to make a mix appropriate for London in December. He was piling and hanging the remaining clothing when Martinez knocked.

"I'm supposed to use your luggage?" she questioned upon entry.

He motioned her to the now-empty suitcase on his desk. "Looks like regular luggage, right?"

She knocked on the hard-shell. "Top-of-the-line, were I to take a guess," she commented.

"This case is made of a mix of Kevlar and polycarbonate, rendering it bullet resistant—roughly equivalent to 3A body armor," he started spouting specs. "More importantly, it has concealed compartments in which you can place your disassembled firearm and holster. This allows us to always be armed if we see the need." He showed her how to access it.

"In addition, if you move this"—Wilson twisted one of the internal support rods—"and pull it out, you'll find a collection of listening devices—bugs, if you will." He inclined the extracted rod and a handful of discreet electronics fell into his palm, along with something about the size of a memory stick and another piece of equipment that looked like a jack of some sort. "You start transmitting when you press this button on one of the bugs"—he indicated a tiny depressible section on each of the bugs—"and the information comes into the home unit you keep with you. You can jack into pretty much about anything using the companion multijack." He mated the two units, demonstrating the various jack options.

Martinez fought the urge to smile as Wilson continued, sounding more and more like an infomercial. "How far do they reach?" she inquired to show she was listening.

"They're supposed to be reliable to about a mile, depending on terrain, but I never try to push more than half a mile unless I have to. The longest I've gotten in the field is twice that."

Wilson replaced the bugs and the internal support rod. "Finally, we have these two little nasties." He slid his hands to the bottom of the luggage and depressed a catch near the wheels. A thin blade popped out into his hand. "There's another on the opposite side," he noted, raising the blade so Martinez could see it clearly. "They're mostly carbon fiber with a bit of metallic glass—don't ask, I don't understand it either. But it makes them damn near unbreakable, even if they don't hold an edge for very long. They are not designed for continuous use. If you're pulling these guys out, you're in a bind and need to get away quick."

Martinez eyed the razor-sharp blade. "I'm assuming these go through security without any problems?"

"Correct. The concealed firearm compartment has covert films that make them seem harmless." He pointed to a section. "This will look like toiletries on their scanners. When you pack, be sure to place your toiletries here. If they stop to search you for some reason, the chances that they'll detect a minute difference in the shapes of the toiletries on the scanner verses the shapes in the bag are slim. The human brain puts things into categories and then forgets about them. They see 'toiletries' on the screen and they see 'toiletries' in the suitcase, so there's not a problem in their mind. It's a remarkably strong psychological trait used by magicians—the Penn & Teller type."

Martinez noted the space for later. "Anything else I need to know before I get my stuff from the hotel and head out to the airport?"

Wilson nodded and unlocked one of his desk drawers. He pulled out an old metal WWII ammo box, from which he withdrew a smaller cardboard ammo box. "This isn't your typical ammunition," he explained, opening the box and handing over one of the 9x19s to Martinez. "They're a mixture of silver, copper, and iron; as you can see, each has four different symbols on it etched in gold."

She turned the cartridge over in her hand. "I recognize the symbol for 'banish' from Chloe and Dot's *Symbolic Dictionary*, but I don't know the other three."

"They're all 'banish,' but from different cultures: Babylonian, Latin, Norse, and Greek. I have others for different continents, but since we're heading to Europe, these will probably be the most efficacious if we need them."

"I thought symbols didn't have power unless you've

'subtexted' them?" she puzzled.

"The symbols don't have to mean anything to us as long as your targets recognize them," he explained. "We just have to pull the trigger and hit them."

"That I can do," Martinez said confidently. "Better to have and not need, than to need and not have."

Wilson broke out with the first genuine laugh she'd heard from him. "Kafka, Martinez? How unexpected."

"Kafka?"

"The quote; that's from Kafka's *The Metamorphosis*, I believe. He was a magician, and not the Penn & Teller type. The rumor is that a transformation spell gone wrong was his inspiration for Gregor Samsa and that famous first line."

"Sorry, never read it. That's just something my mom use to say a lot," she said offhand before returning to the matter at hand. "So, these bullets…made in house, I take it?"

"We used to but it ended up being more expensive. Now we use a custom ammunition manufacturer in Vermont who coordinates with a jeweler to get everything to spec. Each cartridge costs us about twenty dollars outsourced, but there's no cheaper way to get precisely what we want."

Martinez whistled at the figure. "So don't get trigger happy with these."

"On the contrary, if you are fighting something that doesn't belong here among people, take as many shots as you need to send them home," Wilson corrected her. "We do have regular bullets as well, of course; you'll stick with those at first while you're with me."

"So who adds the magic?" she asked, putting it back in the case.

"*That* we do in house. We don't have time for you to meet our armorer today, but he'll be flattered that you liked his luggage."

He looked at the clock and handed over the empty suitcase. "Time to hit the road. I'll meet you at the gate."

Chapter Eleven

London, UK
29th of December, 8:30 a.m. (GMT)

Wilson woke to the piercing shrill of the alarm and experienced that brief moment of discombobulation he always had when he stayed in hotel rooms. They all blurred together, thousands of similar rooms with clean, white starched sheets and fluffy pillows. The only difference was which side of the bed the clock was on. He reached for the alarm and stretched his shoulders; at least this hotel was adequately soundproofed to the point where he could just barely hear the airplanes taking off.

He reoriented himself as the fuzziness of slumber passed, recalling the plane ride over the Atlantic. There had been plenty of time to review the case files Leader provided, and Wilson envied Martinez. Not only was she a faster reader than him, she had no problems dozing off as the sky darkened. She looked younger when she was sleeping—the wariness around her eyes vanished.

He was never able to sleep well on a long flight, and instead peered out the window as the moon shined off the Atlantic six and a half miles below, running the case over in his head. No matter how he'd tried, he couldn't find any connections among the victims other than occupation and gender—ages were different, religions were different, and even politics were different, although they all tended toward the conservative side of their respective countries' spectrums. Eventually, Wilson had surrendered to Mozart's 44th when the lights of Ireland came into view, no wiser than before he left Detroit.

Sometimes he'd wake up after a bout of hard thinking with a new lead that miraculously came to him during the night, but today was not one of those days. He smoothed back his bed head and settled for in-room coffee while he packed—DCI Jones from the Criminal Investigation Department would be here soon enough.

Assigned as their liaison, Jones was supposed to meet them in London and escort them to their next hotel, closer to the scene of the most recent death, and then to Hindon House itself. He'd never worked with the man before, but if he was true to DCI form, he would be put out by the request. He'd made arrangements with Martinez to be at least ten minutes early to alleviate tensions early on and was pleased to see she was already downstairs working her way through breakfast—a full English—when he arrived.

"These things are huge!" she exclaimed as he sat down. "I wouldn't have ordered it if I'd have known."

"The Brits do breakfast right," Wilson affirmed, pushing his luggage out of the way and joining her.

"You want anything?" she nudged and rotated her sundry plates toward him. "I haven't touched the toast and only took one bite out of whatever that black thing is. It's not for me."

"It's called black pudding. It's made of blood and um… oats, I believe. I'm not a fan either," Wilson replied, taking one of the proffered slices of toast, now regretting his decision for sleep over food—they hadn't gotten to the hotel until almost one in the morning. He'd just finished the first slice and was going for the second when a tall, paunchy man in his late fifties entered the room. His face was taut and mildly annoyed, but he wiped it away once he located them at their table.

"Agents Wilson and Martinez?" he asked with a raised eyebrow.

They rose. "That would be us. You must be DCI Jones. So nice to meet you!" Wilson greeted him enthusiastically.

He nodded and shook their extended hands. "I have to say, I've never met Interpol agents before. I thought Interpol just facilitated cooperation between law enforcement agencies among different countries."

"You're not mistaken," Wilson responded, offering him a seat at the breakfast table, which Jones accepted. "There are very few Interpol agents, and we're only sent in with an assistive investigative capacity. Neither my partner nor I have arrest authority in any country other than our own. We're here to help you with any additional information you may require, and provide two more sets of trained eyes to view the problem from the structural framework of the larger interrelated question, rather than on the lone occurrence in the singular locale."

While Wilson gave the professionally jargoned "not here to step on anyone's toes" disclaimer, Jones did a quick assessment as detectives do when meeting someone new. The DCI was subtle enough about it, although both Salt Mine agents could tell his opinion regarding their avoidance of the black pudding. "Well, that explains it. I'm sorry to say I don't keep up with Interpol as well as I should—there's rarely anything in Buckinghamshire that would draw such attention. I was called last night regarding your arrival, and I'm supposed to take you to the scene of the recent unexplained death of Carlmon Grollo of Brockham Laboratories."

"That is correct," Martinez spoke up. "There are things that we simply can't get from a file regarding the death in your jurisdiction, things that someone with local knowledge may find quite obvious. When we interview people, we'd like you to be there to let us know if we're missing something culturally. We've also brought information regarding the four other deaths that have drawn our attention to this one. We'd appreciate any insight you have in the matter once you've had a chance to read them."

Wilson was impressed at her impeccable delivery; he would have believed she was being utterly sincere. *Need to remember that tone*, he made a mental note regarding their future interactions. DCI Jones perked up once he understood that he was there for his expertise, not just to play chauffeur. "Naturally, I'll help in any way I can," he said magnanimously. "We should get going and leave before the worst of traffic, if you're finished with breakfast."

Martinez waved her napkin like a white flag. "The full English has defeated me."

Wilson gladly took the back seat and let Martinez do her thing. She told the DCI she had never been to England before but always wanted to, which left Jones wide open to narrate and expand on his home country as they left London. She commented on her affinity for BBC shows, particularly the classic mysteries, which made Jones smile—everyone is proud of their country, and praising it makes them think better of you. If the DCI had any reservations about working with the pair, they were gone by the time they reached Buckinghamshire an hour later.

"I've arranged for the housekeeper, Mrs. Linda Sharpe, and the cook, Ms. Aisling Moloney, to be at Hindon House when we arrive," Jones outlined the day's itinerary. "The son decided to holiday on Ibiza after the funeral. The house has been closed since the wake," Jones informed them.

"That seems rather heartless," Wilson piped up from the back seat. "The file said that he was one of three inheritors of the rather massive estate, his part being the property and a sizeable trust for him and its maintenance."

"That's correct. There were some donations to various charities, but the majority of the estate passed to him. It may seem cold, but the kid was pretty broken up about the whole thing. King Edward's School closes for two weeks during the holidays, so his only options were to stay alone in the house or go live with his mother…whom he's not fond of, to say the least. There's been more than one physical altercation between them."

"Family is not always a postcard picture in our line of work," Wilson candidly asserted. "Is there intent to sell the property?"

Jones snorted. "Not in the least! Once acquired, these old estates stay in the family—the only time they're sold is when the owners are teetering on bankruptcy, which the young Mr. Grollo most certainly is not." He exited the M40 for High Wycombe and added for Martinez's benefit, "It's an English trait that all the television shows get right. A lot of foolishness happens among the established families because of it."

"Does the Grollo family have a long history here?" she asked for clarification.

"Oh no, they're Italian immigrants. They've only been in the area for four generations." Wilson stifled a snicker about four generations being "immigrants" as Jones continued. "They're new money; they leveraged themselves to penury to put the deceased through proper schooling, and then got lucky.

Grollo bought Hindon House when Brockham Laboratories hit it big about a decade ago. Speaking of which, there she is."

Jones pointed at a massive house at the top of a small hill. It loomed over a spacious lawn dotted with ash, oak, and willow trees. A long paved driveway wound toward the house and turned into gravel where two late-model cars were parked to the side of the central fountain in front of the house. "Looks like the cook and housekeeper are early."

"We could stop there first and check into our hotel later," Martinez suggested.

"No need—it's not more than a mile away. We'll be in and out in fifteen minutes, and we're not due at Hindon for twenty," Jones remarked, keeping the car on the main road.

True to his word, the Bell, Book, and Candle Inn popped into view a minute later, a large brick building containing ten guest rooms with an attached pub. As soon as Wilson saw the reservation details, he knew someone in the Salt Mine was having fun—it wasn't every day that he was booked to stay somewhere named after the old Roman Catholic excommunication ritual. But when he saw the large movie poster of Jimmy Stuart and Kim Novak in the entryway, he had the last laugh.

Jones chatted with the owner while Wilson and Martinez deposited their bags in their rooms. In fifteen minutes' time, they were pulling into the gravel drive outside Hindon House. The massive wooden doors were at least twice their height, and their grand scope was only accentuated by the slight woman who answered the doorbell.

Dressed casually with her light brown hair pulled back into a short ponytail, she looked more like a student on winter break than a cook for such a grand estate. "So nice to see you again, DCI Jones," she greeted him in a thick Northern Irish accent and more familiarity in her airy tone than Jones was comfortable with.

"And you as well, Ms. Moloney," he addressed her with more formality. "This is Agent Wilson and Agent Martinez from Interpol."

"Interpol—who'd have thought Mr. Grollo's strange death would bring international attention!" she exclaimed. "Please come in. I've got the kettle on, and Linda's waiting."

"That's Mrs. Sharpe to you, Aisling!" an older woman's voice called from the back of the house. Moloney rolled her eyes and welcomed everyone inside, closing and locking the giant door behind them. The house felt different after her employer's death, and she took any small measure she could take to make it feel more secure.

Moloney led them through the impressive foyer into the back of the house, where an older plump lady was drinking tea at a long wooden table. "Hello, DCI Jones. These must be the two agents you spoke of."

"Mrs. Sharp, these are Interpol Agents Wilson and Martinez," he repeated for her benefit. The housekeeper gave them a once over as they shook hands. The cook stood back and watched for Sharp's assessment—she put good faith in the housekeeper's keen eye and gut instinct.

"Please do take a seat," Sharp invited them to the table. "Aisling, tea for everyone?" she ordered with a question. "What can we do for you today?"

"Agents Wilson and Martinez have some questions for you…both of you," Jones added, projecting his voice so that Ms. Moloney could hear. "There've been some other deaths in different countries, and they're gathering information to determine if they're connected or just coincidental."

"No such thing as coincidence, my gran used to say," Moloney proclaimed with a full tray.

Wilson flipped open a notebook, mostly for their benefit. Having the right props was part of the act and put people at ease. "Do either of you remember anything unusual about Mr. Grollo's behavior prior to the event?"

"He wasn't eating like he used to," the cook attested before Sharpe could get in a word. "He usually wanted me to cook all sorts of pasta dishes for him, but he hadn't asked for a single one in the week before he died. A whole week without a single *Cacio e Pepe*!" She passed a cup of tea to the DCI, sugared and milked to his preference; she never forgot how someone took their tea.

"Was he on a diet?" Martinez proposed.

A knowing look came over Moloney's face as she readied another cup. "Mr. Grollo had a healthy appetite and didn't exactly need to watch his figure to attract the ladies."

"Aisling!" Sharpe rebuked her.

"I'm not speaking untruths!" she objected. "Sugar or milk?" she asked Martinez.

"One lump and just a splash, thank you," she went along with niceties and let the scene play out.

"We're only here to help," Wilson interjected. "The best you can do for Mr. Grollo now is give us the whole truth, for his children's sake."

Mrs. Sharpe sighed resignedly. "Yes, he had guests now and then, but they were respectable women. I rarely even had to clean up after them."

DCI Jones's demeanor led Wilson to suspect they were rehashing material he'd already thoroughly covered, so the agent started a different line of questioning, "Did Mr. Grollo always collect art?"

"Oh yes, he was very particular on how I was to clean everything," Mrs. Sharpe responded, glad to be off the subject of paramours.

"I saw some paintings and sculptures in the foyer," Wilson observed. "Did he collect other types of art or maybe old books?" he fished as he signaled no sugar or milk in his tea.

"He had an extensive calligraphy collection," Sharpe affirmed. "He kept it in the closet of his bedroom."

"Calligraphy?" Martinez perked up. "Like illuminated books or something?"

"Oh no, not whole books, just single pages," she attested. "I think they were Asian poems, but I couldn't be sure."

Wilson turned to the DCI. "Were these catalogued in the investigation?"

Jones nodded. "Yes, they were compared with insurance listings. There were a hundred and twenty missing pieces, but nothing valued greater than a hundred pounds each. We've put out notices on them, but given the low-key nature of collectable calligraphy, it's likely things were being bought and sold and not recorded for insurance purposes. People don't keep up on these things; there were also sixty or so pieces that weren't listed in any policy."

"I'd like to see them once the interview is over," Wilson tersely requested.

"Certainly," Jones agreed, if a little befuddled by the agents' interest in something he'd previously deemed inconsequential to the investigation.

Wilson returned to the cook and the maid. "As far as you ladies know, anything else other than calligraphy?"

"No, that's it," Moloney responded for the both of them, which earned her an acute glare from Sharpe. "None of it makes sense. The paintings were his pride and joy. He'd occasionally take a meal here instead of in the dining room, and spend the whole time talking about a new painting he wanted that was coming up for auction. Even if he wanted to kill himself, I can't see him destroying his precious paintings in the process."

Martinez saw an opening. "You have doubts it was suicide?"

Moloney clammed up once she saw her words were actually being taken into account—she was used to people ignoring the stream of consciousness that spilled out of her mouth. "I'm sure I don't know, but what else could it be? If someone had come into the house, wouldn't they have taken them?"

"They say Mr. Grollo destroyed more than half a million pounds worth of art when he died," Mrs. Sharpe chimed in, citing the ubiquitous but unnamed "they." Her empty cup clinking against the saucer as she put it down. "Aisling's right. It just doesn't make any sense. He really did love them."

Chapter Twelve

West Wycombe, Buckinghamshire, UK
29th of December, 1:00 p.m. (GMT)

“Finally, our food!” Wilson muttered under his breath as the waitress appeared, carrying two large plates. Two Scotch eggs with chips for him and fish and chips for Martinez, eager to try the real deal. They hastily cleared a space among the paperwork littering the well-worn wooden table at the Bell, Book, and Candle’s pub.

It had been a busy but productive morning between the interview, the physical examination of the grounds and house, and nearly two hours reviewing Mr. Grollo’s extensive calligraphy collection, taking photos as they went. The pictures had already been sent to Chloe and Dot for identification through the Salt Mine’s secure channels, and Jones’s curiosity with their persistence on the matter had been assuaged by a suitably plausible theory Martinez had whipped up: potentially hidden messages in written art forms. Jones had dropped them off at their lodging to unpack and settle in while he attended to other business, and they had a few hours to kill before their appointment with the ME.

As soon as the food hit the table, they dove in and didn't come up for air until there was nothing left but grease. Wilson was surprised at the amount of food Martinez put away, considering her sizeable breakfast, but he didn't make comment as she let him finish her fries and swapped some of her flaky battered cod for her first taste of a Scotch egg. They pushed the polished dishes aside and, after carefully wiping their hands on the napkins, returned to their files.

Wilson broke the post-meal calorie coma. "I was certain we'd find something in one of the calligraphic pieces; bits of old books rarely fail to deliver the supernatural bullet, if there is one to be had."

"Maybe Chloe or Dot will see something you didn't.."

"If anyone can, they will with *their* memory," he retorted. She gave him a peculiar look and he realized his faux pas. "I never told you they have eidetic memories?"

"No, you did not," she curtly informed him. "It would have been nice to know earlier, but it does explain the sour look Dot gives me when I remind her of something she was supposed to do."

Wilson grinned. "Sorry about that. Dot's capricious at the best of times—best to ride the waves and try not to be in her path when it crashes." Martinez made a note to feed Wilson when he became moody or she needed a favor.

He abruptly cut away from the moment of unguarded

sincerity and returned to business. "If there's something in those documents that I missed, they'll catch it. Have you found anything? Any new connections? I feel like I'm missing something, but I can't put my finger on it."

She shook her head. "We've still got the ME interview," she added optimistically while she checked her watch, "in an hour, but I'm not seeing anything that we didn't already know."

Wilson looked outside at the blackening clouds. "I'm going to go to the store across the street to see if they have any umbrellas. You want one?"

"If you would. It looks like it's going to come down hard."

Wilson walked briskly to beat the weather while Martinez started the unenviable task of methodically putting away the papers, scanning them one last time before they went back into their labeled manila folders. She paused when she noticed something in one of the numerous lab findings that wasn't mentioned anywhere in the ME's report. It was probably nothing, but she did a quick search on her phone and made a mental note before tucking it away.

*****

The drive to Slough was noisy from the downpour. "We don't get hard rain like this very often," DCI Jones spoke loudly. "Most of our precipitation is drizzle or mist. This isn't our typical December rain." It struck both agents as something particularly British to apologize for the weather, and they nodded in comprehension. They didn't say much for the remainder of the drive, having nothing to say that warranted yelling at each other over the din.

The clouds sputtered out just before they parked behind the concrete monstrosity that was Slough Hospital. "Dr. Brinston's a peculiar fellow," Jones warned them as they entered. "It'll look like he's wandering sometimes, but give him free rein and you'll see he has a point, and it's usually a good one. He prefers to be the only loquacious one in a crowd, but if he asks you anything, please feel free to answer directly."

"Will do," Wilson answered diplomatically. He understood the desire to preserve a good working relationship with a colleague who has their quirks.

Jones led them through the maze of hallways, past the single security guard, and down into the basement morgue. He paused briefly in front of the doors before opening them, releasing a foul smell that heralded the sight of the large room with its six metal tables evenly spaced in the center.

Dr. Brinston was bent over the far table, occupied by a corpse in an advanced state of decomposition. Without turning or missing a beat, the ME greeted his expected guests, "DCI Jones! If you would be so kind as to wait, I'll be there in a moment. I assure you, closer proximity does not improve the smell."

"Certainly! We'll be outside," he voiced with relief and

escorted the agents back into the corridor. Martinez kept her composure while Wilson mentally acknowledged that it was bad, but he'd smelled worse.

They hovered in the hall and heard the running water splash prodigiously in the metal sink on the other side of the door. A few minutes later, Dr. Brinston emerged, dressed in new, clean scrubs.

"Thank you for your consideration, Dr. Brinston," Jones said appreciatively. "These are Agents Wilson and Martinez from Interpol."

"Ah, yes, pleased to meet you," he greeted them perfunctorily. Wilson put forth his hand, but the ME refused to shake, saying, "It's best if we don't; trust me. If you'd follow me, I've got the information in my office."

He led them down the hallway to the small room, just barely big enough for the four of them. On the table was a thin manila folder. "Humbling to consider that so many lives end with little more than a few pieces of paper," he spoke to no one in particular as he sat down. "Not so with Mr. Grollo, however! His is a complicated matter, not least because of the millions of pounds involved."

"His life insurance policy will not pay out in the event of a suicide," Jones said as an aside to Martinez and Wilson.

"But there is plenty of money to settle and distribute in his estate," Martinez replied.

"Nothing brings out people's true colors like a death,"

Brinston suddenly declared. "But it isn't the money that bothers DCI Jones, is it?" He directed an aside to Martinez and Wilson. "DCI Jones believes there was some sort of foul play but has no evidence to support it, while I believe it was suicide."

"Which you also have no evidence to support," Jones added.

"True, true, but the lack of contrary evidence provides my opinion some greater support, does it not?" he asked rhetorically. Wilson and Martinez watched the volley between the two seasoned players—this was not their first verbal bout.

"You have your methods; I have mine," Jones asserted neutrally. Brinston laughed and slapped his thigh. "I know you, Jones. You feel like there's something wrong, but you've no reason to think so."

"It certainly is an unusual case," Martinez sought to gain consensus. "And I had a question that I don't think was asked before." This brought both the DCI and ME up short. "I was looking through the expected ranges in the blood report and noticed that the deceased's ketones were rather elevated when compared to the printed expected range. Why would that be?"

Wilson fought back a smile. *She knows how to work 'em, doesn't she?* The more he watched her guide the interactions between people, the more he approved.

"Well, that could be attributed to any number of things," the ME began, "but as Mr. Grollo was diabetic, it is most likely related to that."

"Wasn't he on medication and the condition well controlled?" she pressed.

Dr. Brinston looked down at his paperwork, double-checking his memory. "Yes, he was Type II, not on insulin but managed via oral therapy. Are you putting forth the idea of some sort of diabetic ketoacidosis occurring that drove him to eat paintings?" he blasted his voice with a hefty dose of incredulity.

"Oh no, I'm not trying to suggest anything," Martinez responded. "I just found it odd that there was no mention made of it elsewhere in the report or in any of the other files."

Pride assuaged, Brinston shifted into educator mode. "Elevated ketones are byproducts of the body burning something other than carbohydrates. It is either measured in the urine or blood, and is particular concerning with diabetics as it can lead to death when the body has insufficient insulin."

Brinston glanced over the other lab values, talking his way through them. "His A1C showed adequate control of his blood sugars in the last three to four months and he wasn't taking a class of medication that can sometime cause euglycemic diabetic ketoacidosis. There were no signs of metabolic acidosis, and his other chemistries were generally within acceptable range. So while his ketone readings were mildly elevated from the lab's determined range of 'normal,' it didn't seem significant in regard to his diabetes, specifically the threat of DKA."

"So it's high, but not that high," Martinez commented to Brinston's delight—he did so love a willing pupil.

"Precisely."

"But it also happens after someone hasn't eaten in a long time, right?" Martinez led the ME down her line of thinking.

"That is correct. It can happen during weight loss and fasting, but again, at mildly elevated levels. Basically, your body switches from consuming carbohydrates to fats after roughly three days without food, or without food that contains significant amounts of carbohydrates. You have probably heard of what's popularly called a keto diet? Although the public names them as such, they are more accurately described as low carbohydrate diets that use protein as the primary food source. A true ketogenic diet is nearly all fats, and they're almost exclusively something prescribed by a physician.

"So is it possible that Mr. Grollo hadn't eaten for a long time prior to his death?" she posited.

Brinston thought for second, weighing things in his head. Eventually he conceded, "Yes, it's possible. None of his medications would have caused hypoglycemia without the intake of food, and there wasn't anything else in his stomach." He looked down at his notes again. "The large intestine was low in fecal matter, although not enough that I thought it overtly unusual. The ample presence of fiber was more of note, as I recorded."

"What kind of fiber, Dr. Brinston?" Wilson jumped in.

"Pardon?" The ME was taken aback by the question.

"Can you tell what kind of fiber? Could it have been paper?" Wilson clarified his inquiry and the eyes of Jones and Martinez lit up.

"There were more than a hundred pieces of calligraphy unaccounted for in the estate. Could he have been eating those as well?" Jones quickly filled in the gaps for the ME.

Brinston squinted and looked up. "I suppose it could have been paper, but I didn't do any tests on it. If there were other materials present—inks, for example—we could possibly test for that. Please give me a second." He reached for his phone and made a quick call to the lab. They waited silently until he finished.

"You're in luck, DCI Jones. The lab still has a stool sample—they sometimes hold materials regarding a suspicious death for several weeks before they properly dispose of them. We'll be able to run some tests and find out if the ingested fiber is your missing calligraphy. Be thankful it's the holidays; at normal times with a full processing staff, the samples would have been long gone." He put his phone back into his pocket and goaded him with a slight smile. "Still think it wasn't suicide?"

"I have my reservations, yes," Jones firmly but respectfully replied. "When will we get the results on the fiber test?"

"It'll probably take them a few days, perhaps longer due to the New Year's holiday. I could call and expedite matters, if you'd like."

DCI Jones glanced at Wilson and Martinez. "I'm sure they'd appreciate all the speed that we could provide."

"In that case, let's see if I can get it tomorrow," the ME said, reaching back into his pocket.

Once they were well outside ear shot, Jones muttered "Suicide?" under his breath. "From all descriptions, he was a busy, contented, and extremely wealthy man."

"The heart of a man is never truly known by others," Wilson remarked.

"What if it was just an accident, like an overdose?" Martinez suggested

"Overdose?" Jones repeated as they wended their way through the Slough Hospital's white corridors.

"Yeah, maybe he didn't mean to kill himself; he just couldn't stop," she conjectured.

"Couldn't stop eating paintings?" He stopped in the middle of one of the halls to look at Martinez. "You're saying he was addicted to eating strange things?"

She shrugged and held up her arms. "I don't know, but it explains everything—how the pieces in his stomach started off small and got progressively larger until he was trying to swallow entire strips, which killed him."

Jones was troubled but mulled it over, prompting Martinez to continue her theory, "Using safety scissors to cut a painting—isn't that indicative of a strained mental state? I know I'd use a chef's knife over kid's scissors, if for no other reason than ease of use. According to the housekeeper, they were from when his kids were young, and he kept them in the...what did she call it...? The 'bits and bobs' drawer. Imagine the state of desire that would prompt him to grab those from a nearby drawer instead of walking to the kitchen and grabbing a knife. Or better yet, a real pair of kitchen shears."

Martinez could tell that Wilson was already aboard with her idea, his face wolfish in the florescent light. Jones was more hesitant. "That's all dependent upon it being paper fiber in his bowels. Even then, why change from paper to paintings?"

"To continue the metaphor, perhaps he was upping his dose," Wilson put forth. "The calligraphy wasn't very valuable. The paintings were. Perhaps there was some sort of need to increase the transgressive value of the action. Perhaps the act of consumption was related to the perceived value of the consumed goods."

"There's a whole handful of 'perhapses' in that, Agent Wilson," the DCI objected. "And even if your theory is right, that doesn't really get us closer to the reason it happened."

Wilson nodded. "True, but if my hunch proves correct, it's something that Agent Martinez and I can apply to the other potentially related cases. There may be something in one of *those* cases that provides the reason for Mr. Grollo's incomprehensible behavior."

Chapter Thirteen

West Wycombe, Buckinghamshire, UK
30th of December, 2:30 a.m. (GMT)

Wilson had just finished loading his gear when he heard a soft knock on his door. "It's me," a quiet whisper came from the other side. He cracked the door and saw Martinez in the hallway, dressed in her darkest clothes but not completely black like his. He waved her in and shut the door behind her.

Her reassembled weapon weighed heavy in her holster. She didn't relish the idea of illegally carrying a gun, but Wilson insisted on it—if there was something supernatural at work, it was vital to be appropriately armed. At his suggestion, she'd spent some time after dinner digitally walking the local area using satellite and ground-level imaging readily available on the internet even though the pictures were out of date. He'd reasoned that in smaller places like this, it was unlikely much had changed since they were taken, especially if you were just familiarizing yourself with where to run in case things went FUBAR. It was the first time she'd intentionally digitally reconnoitered a target, and she started to understand why some nations weren't keen on having that data readily available.

Although armed, Wilson had stressed this was a no engagement situation for her unless her she believed her life depended upon it. She was instructed to flee at the first sign of detection and rendezvous at a small park nearby if she thought it unwise to immediately return to the inn.

"Are you ready?" Wilson asked as he slid the pack over his shoulders.

"As ready as I'll ever be," she answered nervously.

He flashed a brief humorless smile and tilted his head toward his door. "Welcome to the life of a spy."

They carefully made their way out of the Bell, Book, and Candle via his window. The clouds of earlier had passed and they walked silently, single file in the cold light of the full moon. It was bright enough to cast shadows, and Wilson's was humpbacked from the backpack he wore. The temperature continued to drop to the point of frost and the rare step would elicit a small crunch whenever either of them trod upon an invisible thin crust of newly forming ice.

They made their way to Hindon House, taking the route previously scouted out earlier in the evening under the guise of an after-dinner constitutional. It was time to go off-book and give the old house a "thorough metaphysical look-see," a phrase Martinez would have never expected Wilson to use. Unbeknownst to Martinez at the time, Wilson had taken the liberty of carefully disabling the lock and alarm on a narrow bathroom window when he used the facilities during their interview of the cook and housekeeper.

They approached the manor from the nearby copse of ash trees, treading carefully and slowly under the dim branches. A few dark leaves refused to surrender their hold to the branches, casting mottled shadows on the ground. They paused on the edge of the grove, watching the manor for a good ten minutes before moving toward the unlocked and disarmed bathroom window.

With a quick rush, they were across the lawn and up and over into the bathroom. They clicked on their small lights and crept to the front door and the security panel. Wilson pulled out his phone and tapped a few buttons. He waited for confirmation before placing it carefully atop the panel. "That's all it takes. I'm jamming the radio frequencies used by the sensors throughout the house. We've got about two hours of power, so let's make the best of it. First, to the calligraphy."

Wilson thought her theory that Grollo was under some sort of compulsion was a good one, and if that was magical in nature, it stood to reason there would be traces of it where the calligraphy was stored: the large walk-in closet in the master bedroom. He searched through his pack filled with various small containers, each individually wrapped in thick velvet for silence as well as protection. He extracted an ornately carved cylindrical wooden box and deftly opened it with a twist, revealing a white powder within.

"This is salt, a particularly useful substance when it comes to containing or neutralizing magic, but in combination with this," he withdrew a small ivory tube etched with silver sigils, "we can use it to detect magical residue."

"All we need to do is load it with salt and blow the salt through the tube into the area to be inspected," he explained and looked around the closet. "Which of these drawers do you think contained the 'missing' calligraphy?"

"The closest one," Martinez indicated without hesitation. "It was only half full when we first looked, and human nature is to completely fill the closest containers first and then work your way to the farthest."

"That sounds reasonable," he concurred and handed her the ivory first and then the salt. "One warning—do not inhale the salt."

Martinez paused midway through loading the tube. "Why?"

"Breathing in salt is always a bad idea, but think of it as magical glass blowing. The system is designed to disperse the energy out to a wide area and sucking it in would concentrate it in your lungs."

Satisfied with the analogy, she continued packing the fine grains. "Don't breath in salt, magic or otherwise—got it."

Wilson got out of her way and highlighted the target area with his flashlight. She turned her head to the side and took a deep breath before blowing a cloud of powder centered on the open drawer.

"What now? she queried, handing the tube back to Wilson.

"We wait for the salt to settle. If the even distribution holds, then there's nothing magical going on. But if we see a pattern or an anomalous distribution shake itself out, we have confirmation of a magical force. If we're really lucky, it'll match something in our signature database and we'll know who or what is powering the magic," he explained in a low voice even though the house was empty. Martinez kept her eyes on the salt and tried not to think about Wilson's use of the word "what."

"Why are we using a magical ivory tube if all magic is—and I'm using Dot's words—just shit?" she whispered to Wilson while they waited.

"The saltcaster is a minor magic with high utility, and the price paid to use it so small, it's almost negligible."

"Price?" She did not like that word.

"Nothing's free, Martinez, and this job can take more than you want to give," he stated cryptically. "Karmically speaking, this is something akin to stubbing your toe in the middle of the night or a dropped piece of toast landing buttered-side down—annoying but hardly threatening." His attempt to reassure her made her even more suspicious; Wilson was not the comforting type. In the dim light of the backside of their flashlights, his face looked decidedly untrustworthy, and Martinez swiveled hers to Wilson to gauge his sincerity.

"Watch where you are pointing that thing!" Wilson squinted and raised his hand to block the beam of light. Martinez moved her flashlight away and mumbled a semi-apology. "I wouldn't put anything remotely serious on you without you agreeing first," he clarified as he closed his eyes to reset his night vision. "If you're worried about the negative karma you've acquired, do something good to balance it out—volunteer on your day off, give the rest of your sandwich to a stray, donate to a charity."

"So *that's* why HR had me make a list of charitable organizations," Martinez finally put two and two together. Onboarding for the Salt Mine had involved a series of bizarre questions and hoop jumping.

"Look at that," she whispered in awe as the salt shimmied across the drawer, sorting itself into a pattern. It was like watching grains on a resonance board, or iron dust shift around a magnet.

Wilson took a step forward to interpret the pattern. "You see how it circles here"—he pointed to the center—"but then lines up along the edge of the floor where the salt is thinner?"

Martinez nodded. "What's that mean?"

"It means we've still got a long way to go. Whatever magic was here is very faint. I bet that it was never actually here in Hindon House to begin with, and this is a residual echo of whatever magic compelled Grollo to eat his art," he speculated as he reached for his cell and remembered it was in use elsewhere. "Can you take a picture of it with your phone?"

Before Martinez had a chance to reply, Wilson suddenly jumped backward like a cat that saw a cucumber and the light from his flashlight jerked erratically across the wall and ceiling of the deceased's bedroom. Martinez instinctively put her hand on her Glock and swept the room for threats with her light. "What is it?" she asked as she cleared the room for mundane threats.

"The salt—it's moving again," he said in a hushed voice, pointing his light back inside the drawer. The lines and swirls that formed the intricate pattern dissolved like cotton candy in the water, and the salt dissipated back into an even distribution, like someone had shook the drawer like an Etch A Sketch. He could barely discern the slightest hint of pattern, but only because he had seen it beforehand. After another few seconds, even that was gone.

"I take it that's not supposed to happen," she surmised, taking a defensive stance while Wilson's attention was focused inside the walk-in.

"Not at all." Wilson's voice had a slight tremble. "It means right at this very moment, someone somewhere is practicing magic to cover their tracks. We're dealing with a magically-educated adversary." Goosebumps formed on Martinez's arms—she never thought she'd say this, but she liked stone-faced Wilson better because unnerved Wilson was freaking her out.

"So what do we do?" she asked over her shoulder.

He took to his feet. "Quickly, down to the drawing room and we'll salt again. Get your phone ready." He dashed down the stairs with Martinez in tow. He struggled to pack the tube with salt while holding his flashlight, and loaded it just as he passed through the doors. He exhaled a large cloud over the spot where the body was found while Martinez had her phone aimed and ready.

They tensely waited for the salt to settle, landing in a diffuse spread. When it failed to move further, Wilson cursed. "We have an enemy, all right—and he, she, or *it* knows we're after them."

Martinez pulled the bits and bob drawer open with her gloved hand and grabbed a pad of post-in notes and a pen. "Draw what you remember before you forget." Wilson applauded her quick thinking and started sketching the shapes and swirls he could summon from his mind's eye. It wasn't as good as photo, but it was better than nothing.

When he was finished, Martinez posited a theory. "Could it have been natural dissipation? It's been almost a month since Grollo died."

"No," he shot down her optimism as he set his bag down and wrapped the saltcaster before putting it away. "Natural dissipation would result in no magical signature. The pattern upstairs had been scrubbed. The evening after we started asking questions, no less. But there is more than one way to skin a cat. If we could get a piece of Grollo's body—"

"I am not going grave robbing," she emphatically interjected. She never thought she would have to say that aloud in her lifetime, but she felt it was best to be crystal clear.

"Me neither," Wilson concurred as he riffled through his bag. "At least not in a foreign country. And requesting the body be exhumed would take too long. Plus, there's nothing to stop stop our magically inclined opponent from scrubbing it once we've exposed it. No, I have a different plan," he said proudly as he produced a long yellow plastic drain snake.

"Is that's standard issue?" Martinez joked to lighten the mood.

"In our line of work, yes," he answered earnestly. He made his way to the master bedroom. "The place has been empty since Grollo's death, and I seriously doubt Mrs. Sharpe snaked the drains on a regular basis."

Martinez was glad Wilson only asked her to hold the plastic bag; she hated messing with drain hair and the smell of slow damp decay was bad enough. Once secured, Wilson retrieved his phone and they made their way back to the inn.

Chapter Fourteen

West Wycombe, Buckinghamshire, UK
30th of December, 8:30 a.m. (GMT)

The dim morning sun beamed in low through the clouds, bathing the pub in a golden glow and casting rich shadows against the dark wood. The only people inside were the inn's few guests having breakfast and its owner tallying last night's consumption and awaiting this morning's restock. Wilson sat at a small wooden table in the corner, dipping his strips of toast into his runny boiled egg with its top sliced off, perched inside an egg cup.

The turn in the case was troubling to say the least. Going up against practitioner using magic to cover up murder by supernatural means was a whole other realm of bad. His disposition hadn't improved when he heard back from Chloe and Dot: there was nothing supernatural about the calligraphy. They had received his sketch of the magical signature found in Grollo's closet, but they hadn't found a match yet.

Wilson was finishing off the last of his boiled eggs and soldiers when Martinez entered the room. "Morning," she greeted him, taking the opposite seat at the bistro table. "Any news?"

"Nothing helpful," he replied as the waitress stopped by their table, depositing a duplicate of Wilson's breakfast in front of Martinez along with a hot cup of coffee. She stirred in a spoon of sugar and bit of milk and savored the first sip.

"I'd ordered earlier," she explained when she finally saw Wilson's puzzled expression. "The full English was nice, but this seemed more reasonable." She waited until the waitress was out of earshot before she brought up work. "Do you have any ideas about what exactly we are dealing with?"

Wilson wiped his mouth with his napkin and pushed his plate to the side. "Assuming that all five deaths are connected and there is a magically-fueled compulsion component, there are a few things it could be. First, there are spells. I should be able to use the hair I acquired from the drain to run some tests once we get back."

"Tests?" Martinez mumbled through a mouthful of egg and toast.

"Every magician leaves a trace of themselves in their magic, and since magic is an entirely personal manifestation, there are a number of esoteric tests that can be performed to find out more about the magic and/or the magician," he elaborated.

"So it's like fingerprints, but more mystical," she summed up as she untopped her second egg and dipped a sliver of toast in the yolky goodness.

The corners of Wilson's mouth upturned. "Something like that. Saltcasting is fine and well, but it relies on matching something in our database, which is limited to what we've already encountered. If the culprit is something or someone new to us, that won't really help us catch them. It would be like trying to find a murderer using their fingerprints when they aren't in the system. The kind of things I can find out with a piece of the deceased will yield information that could be useful regardless of if the magic is new to us. It's something you'll learn to do too, once you've acquired training to become a practitioner of the arts."

"First a supernatural agent, then a magical spy; tomorrow, a wizard," Martinez remarked, tongue-in-cheek. "So last night was basically someone wiping their fingerprints off a murder weapon?"

"Exactly. And if they didn't get around to doing the house until last night, there's a good chance the hair is still good," he explained.

"Because Grollo is already six feet under," she completed his thought.

"An eye or a tongue would have been better, but the hair should do in a pinch," he replied nonchalantly.

On that grisly note, Martinez pushed the rest of her breakfast away and focused on her coffee. "If someone can just wipe down the magic, why didn't they do that right after the murder? Why wait until we start investigating?"

"Because it's costly," he said plainly. "The cover up is more expensive than the crime, and the karmic debt for using magic to kill someone is already high."

"Is karma really a problem if it can be offset—good deeds and all that?"

"Sure," he conceded. "But why spend it on a cover up if the locals are chalking it up to a suicide? If our culprit scrubbed all five murders as a precaution, the cover up would cost more than the crimes."

Martinez's brow furrowed. "I'm afraid you lost me." She drained the last of her caramel-colored coffee and pushed her cup and saucer to the edge of the table for a refill.

"The karmic cost of magical obfuscation is related to the cost of the action itself, and it isn't additive. It's closer to exponential," Wilson explained.

"Which means our target is some combination of desperate, determined, and loaded," she extrapolated and grabbed a piece of toast, giving breakfast another shot. "It doesn't seem right that someone can just buy off the karma of murder-by-magic."

He gave a flippant nod. "Magic is like everything else. Money is power, and power exists to avoid consequences. Behind the creation of almost every major charitable organization is a magician trying to balance the scales for something particularly heinous. Karma may play by its own rules, but don't forget, we're on the board too." Martinez chewed on that along with the last of her toast as the waitress came back to refill their coffees.

"What worries me is the price paid for five murders and the cover-up of at least one scene. It suggests more to come, and they needed to buy themselves more time by throwing us off the scent. Not only do they know how to use magic, they know we police it. Whoever's calling the shots is scheming without apparent concern of the consequences to their own self. Or they're stinking filthy rich and buying off the karma as fast as they can, regardless how inefficient an exchange rate they're getting."

Martinez glommed onto what he was saying. "So we should be checking the news to see if there have been any recent major charitable donations?"

He gave a curt nod. "I've already asked the Mine to put some resources on it. Technically, you don't have to balance the scale immediately—karma can take a while to catch up with you. Personally, I find it's best to do it as soon as possible because sometimes it doesn't dawdle."

She stacked their dishes to the side making it easier for the waitress to remove them before picking up her refreshed coffee. "If it's not a compulsion spell, what else is on the table?"

"It could be a supernatural creature. There are many beings that can delude the senses and trick a person into thinking they're doing one thing while they're actually doing another. Given the geographic dispersal of the victims, I'm inclined to think it isn't an independently acting creature—it's extremely rare for a single creature to travel across continents without some help from a magician. Then, there's magical items."

Martinez raised her eyebrow. "Like the Holy Grail?"

"Not the Grail…we have that. Something like—"

"Wait, you have the Holy Grail?"

"Not me personally, no, but the Salt Mine contains many enchanted items. Most of them are cursed in some way or another."

"The Holy Grail is cursed?" she whispered behind her cup.

Wilson let a small smirk slip. "It's a textbook example of a curse. You think something that kills anything that touches it is holy?"

Martinez had so many questions but Wilson pushed forward on the case. "I was thinking something like Glitonea's Wand, which is still unaccounted for. She was one of the Nine Sorceresses—the only one you've probably heard of is Morgan le Fay. Her wand would confuse the senses and might be able to do something like this—we've never had a chance to study it. Magical items are always the wild card in our investigations."

"So it could be a person, or persons, a creature, or an item?" she summed up, ticking each off a raised finger. "I feel like I'm at the beginning of a twisted game of Twenty Questions."

"That's where we stand. But at least we know it is something that warrants our attention, and it's active and ongoing." He looked at his watch, "We need to get going if we're going to catch our flight back to the Mine."

Chapter Fifteen

Boston, Massachusetts, USA
31st of December, 9:30 a.m. (GMT-5)

"We'll announce the news tomorrow," Charles Roberts weakly croaked. With him were his two oldest friends, Emily Thibodeaux, COO of Detrop Pharmaceuticals, and Martin Phillips, the CFO. They were on the third floor of Roberts's massive brownstone, in his master suite—now converted into a hospice room. Three weeks ago, he had collapsed in front of them, and since then, he'd been put through every conceivable medical test. None provided an answer to his condition—his digestive system was shutting down.

Equally troubling was his desire to consume gold, and the euphoric reaction he had to it. When they conducted neurologic imaging, the MRI and MEG could not have been more telling. At rest, there was nothing abnormal, but when Roberts was allowed to consume half of a gold coin, his brain lit up like a Christmas tree. The neurologists had seen nothing like it before, and the literature drew a blank. They couldn't explain why he reacted to the gold in such a dramatic fashion, but more to the point, it didn't account for why Roberts vomited whenever he consumed anything other than water. After two weeks of fruitless testing, Roberts decided that enough was enough. He was growing weaker by the day, and it was time to put his things in order and accept that, for whatever reason, he was going to die. Soon.

Roberts set a personal survival goal—he always set goals—to live to see his forty-ninth birthday. January 7th was a week away, and he was determined to make it. The intravenous feed pumping him with nutrients and sugars was the only thing that had kept him alive up to this point, that and his two live-in nurses, one of which was always in the room with him. Roberts wryly called them his "escort crew," there to guide him on to the next challenge. He tried to keep his mind off the gold, which consumed his every thought.

Officially, Roberts had taken "personal time," but his nearly boundless charisma and the bustle of the holidays had its limits; the board of directors was getting edgy. Last week, Roberts had dictated a letter explaining to the board and the media of his sickness—never naming what ailed him—and of its seriousness. In his missive, he suggested Thibodeaux become the acting CEO until his return or his death. He'd sat on the letter, hoping that something would change, but now, with the new year knocking at the door, he knew he couldn't wait any longer. He'd built Detrop Pharmaceuticals, and he needed to do right by it and his friends.

Roberts's declaration was welcomed with relief by both Thibodeaux and Phillips, who wanted to get the situation into the public eye. The weight of nebulous uncertainty and futile hope that hung over them these past few weeks had only gotten heavier with each passing day. "I think it's for the best," Thibodeaux concurred, standing by his bed. It was an adjustable metal hospital bed with railings, a cold thing covered in white, crisp starched sheets. She didn't like it—the stark contrast of sterile white and slow, wasting death was too acute—but she swallowed her distaste and focused on her old friend instead. As usual, the railings were up; they kept him from rolling off when his desire for gold overcame his senses. There were restraints—Roberts had demanded them—but he was so weak now that there was no longer a need for them.

"I think you've waited as long as you could, Chuck. I didn't want to believe it, but I think this is the last exit," Phillips conceded, his eyes red with a film of tears behind his glasses. He remembered the rambling conversations they'd had in college, staring up at the changing afternoon clouds. He was stoned out of his mind and Chuck was just high on life and endless possibilities. They'd philosophize that death was nothing more that someone leaving the room and never coming back, how everyone who leaves the room was actually dead until the moment you see them again.

"Don't worry about it, Martin. If there's an afterlife, I'll be waiting for you there. If there's not, well…we did some good, didn't we? We didn't change the world, but we polished it up a bit," Roberts reassured his ginger partner-in-hijinks.

Phillips removed his glasses and wiped away his tears. "That we did, man, that we did. We'll do some more, too. The board's pissed as hell with you right now, but once they find out, they'll shut up."

"I admit, I would like to see the board fume when they find out. My death will ensure the patents get released into the public domain to a big fanfare—they'll be unable to stop it once the media gets hold of the story. I'll become some sort of martyr; the patron saint of pharmaceuticals with a conscious."

"Yep," Thibodeaux clipped the word short, unable to hide her discomfort with the plan. They'd always had a strange relationship, the three of them. They were close friends, competitors, and more than anything else, genuine sounding boards. Their honesty had kept them together through the ebbs and flows of their lives. They didn't always agree, but they had to tell each other the truth—that was the unspoken rule.

Roberts started to laugh, which triggered a coughing fit, violently wracking his frame. They could do nothing for him; he wasn't drinking much water at this point, only sips here and there. The IV kept him adequately hydrated, and the nurse regularly daubed his lips and mouth with a damp cotton swab to keep the skin moist. They waited uncomfortably until it passed, surprised by the smile on his impossibly thin face. "You remember how upset you were about losing four percent,

Martin?" he goaded his CFO.

Phillips recognized his friend's grasp for normalcy and ribbed him gently, "I remember it being forty percent."

"If you put a PR firm on this, you may be able to come out on top. With the right spin, the proper media coverage—I bet they pick the picture of me from the photo shoot in the penthouse of the Custom Tower House—you'll be able to get back your four percent this year," Roberts speculated, his eyes for the briefest moment hinting at the forceful personality he once had been.

"Ha, ha," Phillips responded with equal parts sarcasm and sadness, unable to keep up the ruse of normality. "It's a nice idea, Chuck, but we won't be getting it back. We"—Phillips looked at Thibodeaux for support and a united front—"have decided to release a few more patents in dribs and drabs over the next few years."

Roberts didn't have the energy to lift his head, but he raised his eyebrows; this was news to him. "I should die more often," he joked.

Phillips carefully took his hand. "What I'm trying to say is you were right, Chuck. We're full. It's time to build a bigger table."

Chapter Sixteen

Detroit, Michigan, USA
31st of December, 10:30 a.m. (GMT-5)

The plane violently thumped onto the snow-dusted runway, shocking Martinez out of her half sleep. What had started off as "just resting my eyes" had turned into several hours of sleep as her body crashed from the spike and sudden withdrawal of adrenaline that came with covert operations. No new case files to review to occupy her mind, and the promise of three days off on her return stateside was a recipe for slumber. She had even slept through the pre-landing announcements and bustle.

Beside her, Wilson spent most the flight on his phone, periodically looking over at Martinez. He remembered doing the same thing when he began—the stresses of prior occupations just weren't comparable to the stress on a new covert operative. Every second is tense; even those that don't particularly seem so. Eventually, the operative learns to deal with the pressure or ceases to be an operative, supernatural or not. Martinez had good instincts; he hoped for her sake that she learned how to adapt, as the path to unemployment could be particularly gruesome once you were in the employ of the Salt Mine.

Wilson continued searching various research documents as the plane crossed over the Atlantic. He had a small portable encyclopedia of the supernatural at his fingertips at all times, disguised as files for an old tabletop roleplaying game published decades ago. Were anyone to gain access to his phone, he would just appear to be a fan of an esoteric game, which a quick web search would reveal never really gained much traction when it was released. The Salt Mine had purchased the rights to the game decades ago and ran it as a shell corporation. It's wiki-listing even included a fabricated biography of the current owner, limping along on miniscule sales and minor past glories.

The plane taxied off the frosty runway and mated with the jet bridge seconds after coming to a complete stop. Martinez and Wilson sat out the rush for the exit, waiting until most people had already left to gather their things. Neither of them had pressing business—personal or otherwise—that warranted joining the fray. A few minutes later, they retrieved their luggage from the carousel. With promises to return his luggage on Monday, Martinez joined the blurry-eyed, jet-lagged procession to the parking lot.

As they went their separate ways, Martinez finally let her game face drop as she neared her rented Subaru. She chunked her luggage into the trunk and climbed into the driver's seat, turning on the engine and flipping the heater to full blast. The cold air rushing out the vents hit her face and she reached for the seat warmer, hardly a feature she needed on the west coast but something she had come to appreciate in Detroit. For the first time in her life, she was worried that she wasn't going to be capable for the task ahead, that she was going to fail. She'd never doubted herself before, and she hated that she was doing it now.

She had always excelled at anything she put her mind to—and she wasn't one to only pick low-hanging fruit—but this was a whole other world of strange. She reached for the pendant of St. Michael that shared a chain with a crucifix, both given to her by her mother for protection. Martinez wore them more from sentimentality than from faith, but if magic was real and demons could be trapped in a salt basement, then why couldn't God or an angel be watching out for her?

The click of the blue cold-engine light disengaging called her back to reality. Martinez adjusted the heat now that it was actually blowing warm air and shifted the car into gear. She set off for her hotel, only to find the highway clogged with traffic. She had no patience for gridlock, not today, and exited as soon as she could. She drove aimlessly about the city for hours, lulled by the illusion of progress that movement granted. Detroit wasn't home. She was living out of a hotel, and all her stuff was still in Portland and would be until she found a more permanent living situation. The more she thought about it, the more she liked the idea of buying a house. Having a place to fix up would help keep her grounded when she wasn't working.

Busy hands made for peaceful minds. Maybe she could even get a garden going in summer.

As she drove, she kept one eye out for potential houses, but her worries continued to surface, no matter how many times she batted them away with reason. There had been dozens of Salt Mine agents, and she was as qualified as any of them. She was handpicked from God knows how many others. They knew what it took to be an agent, and they wanted her. A familiar power ballad came over the satellite radio and bolstered Martinez's resolve. The way forward was the relentlessness she'd applied to everything in her life. If she was going to be a Salt Mine agent, she was going to be the best of them.

She caught sight of a soup kitchen and took a sudden turn to circle the block. Once she found a parking spot, she fished out a couple of twenties before shutting off the car. She could use all the good karma she could get.

*****

After saying his goodbyes, Wilson deposited his luggage in his car. Thanks to an accident that shut down all but one lane on I-94, he crawled his way home over the next hour. The 500 was as he left it, and he exited the 911 after the satisfying crunch of the descending garage door. Wilson exhaled deeply, wiping the stress away in the safety of his personal little fortress. He dragged his luggage up the spiral stairway—the only downside of the beautifully enchanted piece of ironwork—and unpacked, setting the hair sample aside for his full attention once everything else was back in place.

He bumped up the thermostat on the fourth floor while he got the laundry started and changed to more comfortable clothing. He needed to warm the esoteric parts of the 500 to a balmy 76° F for the forthcoming ritual. He grabbed a drink and turned his attention to the sample of the former Mr. Grollo. The mat of hair was still damp in the plastic, and that wouldn't do. Wilson tamped down the damp hair with paper towels and then put it into one of his dehydrators, set for two hours. That should ensure it was moisture free and suitable for testing.

With nothing else pressing, he turned on the TV, wrapped himself in a quilt someone's grandmother had made, and watched the first two episodes of a twelve-part documentary about the history of Southeast Asia. He knew little of the ancient history of that part of Asia, and found it fascinating. The ding of the dehydrator brought him out of the spell of the rise and fall of the Kutai, Kalingga, and Tarumanagara Kingdoms. He turned off the TV and checked on the sample; it was a bit drier than it needed to be, but he thought it always better to err on the side of caution. He scooped it into a new baggie and headed into the arcane parts of his residence.

A full three thousand square feet of the 500 was dedicated to his profession. The only entry was behind a cold-iron door inlaid with silver sigils on both sides—Wilson did not want anything to get in, nor did he want anything to get out. It cost several thousand dollars to manufacture, but it couldn't be picked. Four handles had to be manipulated in a particular sequence and manner before the door's lock would release. Anyone who wanted to get into the restricted parts of his residence would be better off trying to punch through one of the walls, but even that would require the use of a jackhammer.

On the other side of the door was a short hallway and two doors. Behind one was a small exercise area he used when he didn't feel like hitting the gym, and in the other was an S&M dungeon, fully stocked with every imaginable device. While he had no interest in S&M, it provided the perfect cover for the unusual door if the 500 was ever subjected to a subpoena, even if it required more dusting than he preferred to maintain the "well-used" look. Bolted into the floor, a massive, ornately carved Saint Andrew's Cross dominated the room. He quickly climbed it and hit a release catch on the very top, freeing the cross from its bolts and sliding it to the left, revealing a dark crawlspace that provided access to his real secret.

Crawling through the darkness, Wilson popped out the other side in a pitch-black room. He closed the trapdoor and walked to the light switches located across the room and within a closed panel, the last of his defenses against accidental intrusion. The flick of a switch flooded the room with soft light, revealing a heavily carpeted study decorated in baroque style. The walls bore hundreds of books in glass-paned bookshelves, but one immediately stood out. Carved from ebony, inlaid with ivory signs and sigils, and paned with solid sheets of quartz, the large bookshelf was mostly empty, containing only twenty-seven books. Wilson retrieved one from its number and brought it to his desk, lit by an Emeralite lamp with a pull of its small chain.

The Recurved Mind of Elliot Smith was printed in 1921 by Foote & Davies Company. It was a biography and case study of a young man driven to insanity during the First World War. Smith claimed to see creatures that were not there—angels and devils—and insisted that the war was a physical manifestation of their spiritual contest. The author, a Dr. Herbert Belangier, kept impeccable and copious records of their sessions, many of which were included in the exhaustive endnotes. It was these passages that Wilson paged through, searching for the doctor's account taken on October 25th, 1919. It was a short note indicating that Patient Smith had taken to repeating a bit of poetry when asked any question:

The tree in winter dreams of spring.
The root in spring dreams of rain.
The leaf in summer dreams of flying away.
And I, in prayer, dream of the smile in the darkness.

Wilson did not know what originally drew him to that particular bit of text, but whatever it was, it had power. He again committed the verse to memory and reshelved the book before walking through one of the two cold-iron doors in his study. His summoning chamber, the largest of his secret rooms, was plainly furnished, containing a single wooden chair used by Cotton Mather during the Salem Witch Trials and a long cabineted table upon which resided many occult objects. Next to the table, a mini-refrigerator cheerfully hummed. Upon the floor, inscribed in silver, were six different types of summoning and protective circles.

Wilson pulled a vial of his blood from the mini-fridge and poured it out into a smaller, darkly stained circle that lay in the center of the area within the thirteen-sided star inscribed by a great circle. He picked up the chair, placed it beside tridecagram, and began. "I summon you," he intoned before repeating the poem of the madman Elliot Smith. "I summon you," he chanted again, and again repeated the poem. Finally, he intoned a third time and the center of the tridecagram filled with whirling, black smoke.

"I am here," declared a voice that wasn't a voice.

"I require service of you," Wilson responded, actively working to keep his tone, face, and body language impassive.

"Where is the sacrifice?" the stridulation droned in response.

"In a circle that is outside your view; it is my blood. I will open it for you now to consume only if you agree." Wilson raised one arm and with a flourish, revealed the previously hidden blood to the demon.

"And you are?" The inquiry, although expected, cut to the core of Wilson. The hair on his arms rose, and his heart rate shot up. The primal part of him—the part of the monkey that didn't descend from the trees—did not want to answer. It did not want, under *any* circumstances, for Wilson to make himself known to the Smile in the Darkness.

"I am David Emrys Wilson," he answered after the briefest of hesitations.

Yellow orange teeth flashed in the smoke, disappearing into the blackness in the blink of an eye. "I taste salt about you, David Emrys Wilson."

Wilson said nothing.

A different set of teeth—this time human, but as long as Wilson's forearm and white as bleached bone—flashed out of the darkness. "You do not taste as a stranger tastes. You have bargained with me before."

"I have."

"And yet no memory remains. You dilute your flesh, dilute your tracks. Why should I bargain with you?" The teeth slinked back into the darkness.

"My blood is all that's offered," Wilson stood firm.

"It is a paltry offering," the swirling smoke ridiculed him.

"It is a paltry task I request," Wilson kept his voice and hand steady.

"You lie," it cast accusations to stir emotion. Wilson gave it no such satisfaction.

"I do not. I seek the name of a magus. I seek you to taste your way to an identity and inform me of the worker behind the work."

The whirling darkness was silent for a moment before it boomed, "Agreed!" A massive jaw—the jaw of a megaladon—coated with Wilson's blood appeared out of the inky black, then smiled. Wilson's blood drained in rivulets, seeping into invisible pores on the massive row of smirking teeth. "Make the smoke for me to taste, and I will tell you what you want to know."

Wilson split Grollo's dried hair into thirteen equal parts and lit a candle, setting a portion aflame at each of the thirteen points in the tridecagram. As they burned, their smoke was drawn into the ebony mist of the Smile in the Darkness. Once all of the hair was burned, Wilson returned to his chair and waited.

The megaladon maw appeared through the haze. "David Emrys Wilson, you seek a name that you should not seek. For if found, it will destroy you."

"Just the name, please," Wilson pressed—the opinion of a demon wasn't to be trusted.

The maw spitefully smiled behind wisps of darkness, relishing the news it had to deliver. "You seek the dying-and-rising god, the liberator, the twice-born, the god that comes. You seek Dionysus."

Chapter Seventeen

Detroit, Michigan, USA
31st of December, 2:36 p.m. (GMT-5)

"So that's what I got," Wilson finished his account to Chloe, Dot, and Leader. They were in Leader's office at his request for a special meeting, something he'd only done a few times previously. They dropped what they'd been doing to join him, despite the fact that most everyone had taken the day off for an extended weekend.

"Dionysus? That's not a name you hear of every day," Dot broke the quiet of the room. All eyes were on Leader.

"Chloe, Dot, summation on Dionysus, please," she requested.

Chloe took point. "Dionysus: one of the Greek gods, parentage uncertain but attributed to Zeus and a mortal woman. His spheres are ecstasy—religious and physical—madness, wine, grapes, and theater. We believe his current form solidified in the Minoan period, although one of the birthing stories has him appearing in ancient Egypt as the son of the Egyptian god Amun."

"He, like all the gods, is an ethereal manifestation of humanity's unconscious. As such, he has powers in relation to the number of his worshipers," Dot continued. "Although he is no longer worshiped, there are still millions of drinkers and the action powers him, even if performed non-religiously."

"And millions of people still ritualistically consume wine every week," Chloe added, garnering a nod of agreement from Dot, "even if the consumption is not in memory of Dionysus in particular."

"Noteworthy abilities?" Leader queried.

"Dionysus can assume any form, change the forms of others, cause insanity, and grant wishes to the worthy—but as with all such magics, they usually have unwanted side effects. He is one of the few who has entered Hades and returned, bringing the dead back to life with him."

"Insanity could be a possible association in this case," Wilson suggested.

"Maybe," Leader responded, "but there's still a lack of motive."

"Perhaps he's upset about the proliferation of drugs? There's less and less of a reason every year to overindulge in wine?" Wilson conjectured.

"You're stretching for that, and you're wrong," Dot retorted bluntly. "Although all of the deceased were in the pharmaceutical industry, none of them were focused on psychoactive medications, and two of them didn't manufacture any at all. And all the recreational illegal drugs are definitely not being made by pharmaceutical companies."

Wilson shrugged in defeat, but took her word for it; he

was no slouch, but he knew he didn't have the memory or processing power she did, allowing her to instantly analyze a theory as bunk or a real possibility. It was one of the many strengths Dot and Chloe brought to the Mine. It had bothered Wilson initially—he was unaccustomed to not being the sharpest tool in the shed—but he came to appreciate it rather than resent it. A little bruised pride was a small price to pay, if it meant he spent less of his time chasing down leads that went nowhere. Having his ideas shot down by Chloe and Dot was a commonplace thing for him now; par for the course.

"Fulcrum, why did you choose the Smile in the Darkness?" Leader inquired curiously, with a very slight note of recrimination in her tone—it was the magic equivalent of using a sledgehammer to kill a cockroach when the bottom of your shoe would have done. Alleviating the karmic debt of summoning Smile wouldn't be cheap, and there was no doubt he would be adding the service to his expense report, although he would have to foot the bill himself to remove his taste from Smile's memory.

Wilson paused for a second before answering her. "I have a gut feeling that something unusual—something *new*—is happening here. It just doesn't feel like a case of a pissed-off wizard, and although Smile scares the hell out of me, it always finds what it's seeking. It's the only reason I'd access such a high-level resource." He couldn't tell if Leader was appeased, but the fact that she said no more about it was a positive sign in his mind.

"I think all we're going to get out of this right now is hasty speculation," she concluded. "Let's do our individual research on Dionysus and see what we can come up with before we reconvene on Monday morning. Chloe, Dot, if you'd join me in the Library, I have some threads I want to unravel. Fulcrum, I want you to speak with Aloysius and see if he knows anything."

Wilson had worked with Leader long enough to pick up on her undercurrent of caution—Aloysius was a good source of gossip, and because of that, he was a good distribution center for misinformation. A little creative fabrication might eventually be in order; anything that could sow confusion in the mind of an enemy they had not yet identified might prove valuable if it came to that. Even though he wasn't thrilled with the prospect of speaking with the magician, especially on New Year's Eve, Wilson nodded in agreement. It was time for a social visit, if for nothing more than to prime the misinformation pump for a later time.

*****

Herman Aloysius Hardwick was a pale, fat man. He had been bald since the age of twenty-eight, and in the three decades since, he'd somehow managed to lose all of his facial hair as well. Aloysius claimed it was part of a bargain that he'd made with a devil, but Wilson suspected he waxed. He sweated profusely and preferred the colors purple, green, and gold, which gave him the appearance of a one-man Mardi Gras krewe on his worst days. He insisted everyone call him Aloysius—he hated Herman, and Mr. Hardwick was his bastard of a father.

He was the owner of 18 is 9, a goth dance club tucked away in one of Detroit's many old warehouses, and was the sole consumer of at least half of the black lights sold in the metro area. His clientele came in all ages, from wee gothettes squeezing into their first black chiffon dress to goths old enough to have "remember when?" conversations with the living dead. When business was booming—and it almost always was—he could be found moved among "his crowd" like a Christmas ornament, the lone patch of color in a sea of black, white, and red. But Aloysius was more than just a successful businessman with poor taste in clothing, he was a practitioner of the arts; 18 is 9 was not only the de facto gathering place of magical wannabees, it was the place where the authenticos stopped by when they were in the neighborhood.

Like many innate magic users, Aloysius discovered his abilities in his teens, and he relentlessly abused them until karma came along and kicked him in the ass. After his second near-death experience, he'd decided that circumspection was needed in his use of magic, even if there was no chance for such bleeding over into other aspects of his life. Even in his youth, Hardwick demonstrated the clear mind and unerring social skills that would later make him a perfect club owner.

As his magical abilities grew with time, he mostly limited their use to helping his business, although he did have his weaknesses, namely charming whoever caught his attention. His efforts were subtle, pushing himself into their minds, turning himself into an option that they wouldn't have otherwise considered. Aloysius liked to think he wasn't overriding someone's free will, just giving them a little nudge, but the end result didn't seem much different.

However, the magician wasn't so considerate when it came to authority figures. His abilities ensured that no law enforcement—local or federal—ever found anything in 18 is 9, even though everyone knew it served alcohol to the underaged. Rivers of drugs also flowed through the establishment, but he kept close watch on the "bad ones" and shut them down as quickly as he saw them. Aloysius loved feeling good and making others feel good—finding an overdose in the bathroom undermined all of that—so he strove to keep his club clean-ish.

Wilson first met Aloysius nearly ten years ago while he was working a case involving an underage prostitution ring—two brothers had gotten their hands on an ancient Hittite ring used by temple prostitutes which made authorities overlook their behaviors, believing them to be legal. The brothers occasionally visited 18 is 9 when they were in the USA, and without Aloysius's assistance, Wilson would have had to take them out to retrieve the ring, a considerably more difficult and expensive resolution that came with a lot more baggage.

Wilson was happy to avoid assassination, but working with Aloysius had been trying. He found him personally distasteful—there was something about the man that deeply rubbed him the wrong way. Maybe it was the way he was always touching people's shoulders, or the way he'd enter the room as if that was the most important thing happening at the moment. Wilson spent the drive over tamping down his aversion; there wasn't a wine bar in the entire state that served more red wine than 18 is 9, so he understood why Leader had sent him—if Dionysus was involved in the current case, it would be the logical place to start looking.

Officially, the 18 is 9 didn't open until ten p.m., but Wilson's persistent knocking brought someone to the door. Behind the metal bars and through the thick glass, he received a solid "Go away!" from the large, shadowy figure.

He flashed his FBI identification and waited.

"Do you have a warrant?" the voice called back after a few seconds.

"No." Wilson responded.

"Then go away!"

"Go tell Aloysius to get his fat butt out of the basement and let me in or I'll get a warrant and then instead of just talking, he'll end up paying for my time," Wilson threatened.

The dark blur moved away from the door, and Wilson put away his identification, assuming his message was percolating its way to the magician himself. Although Wilson found the tough-guy routine extremely tedious, posturing and threat-making were a large part of the job because they worked. Popular entertainment had propped up the notion of the intelligent and methodically logical criminal, but Wilson had yet to encounter one of the fabled rational actors who put aside ego and emotion when it came time to make decisions. Criminals like that only existed in fiction or perhaps in boardrooms, where they had to at least make sure their schemes remained legal. *Probably not even them,* Wilson thought on it longer. *Their wealth and connections push the threshold of failure further back, but that doesn't necessarily mean they are any less impetuous.*

The cold wind was just starting to cut through him when a series of metallic thuds indicated his message had been received. The door eventually opened to three hundred pounds of muscle that towered over Wilson at a full six-foot-six. "Boss said you can come in. You can wait at the bar in the Nostradamus Room. I'll show you the way." Wilson didn't need the escort, but doubted that would dismiss the security, so he played along. The giant led him through the entryway, past the alabaster statues glowing in the black lights—*Don't they ever turn them off?* Wilson wondered—and through to the back of the massive club. He'd only been here a few times when it was packed, and he was sure it held close to a thousand people, the fire marshal's limit of five hundred be damned. He was eventually deposited in a leather-lined booth decorated with metal strips and a large scratchboard upon which someone of considerable talent had etched a mortuary scene.

"The boss will be here in a bit. Would you like a drink?" the bouncer asked.

"Just sparkling water, please," Wilson responded. The giant grunted in response and left, only to return shortly with the water and the indomitable Herman Aloysius Hardwick trailing in his shadow.

"Agent Wilson! So lovely to see you again!" he greeted, putting his left hand on Wilson's shoulder before oozing into the seat opposite him. He was dressed conservatively for Aloysius—a purple suit with a green shirt and a gold silk tie.

"Nice to see you again as well, Mr. Hardwick," Wilson lied.

"Oh, do call me Aloysius! I told you last time you're entirely too formal."

"Aloysius, then," Wilson conceded, closely watching the fat man's hairless face.

"What can I do for you this fine day?" he asked to Wilson's surprise. The past few times he'd been at 18 is 9, he felt like he'd been chatted up before they got down to business.

"I'm looking for information."

Aloysius's eyes lit up, the wrinkles smoothed, and his hairless eyebrows lifted. "I'm always at the ready for an information exchange."

"I was hoping you'd offer what you know out of the kindness of your heart," Wilson responded.

"Oh, Agent Wilson!" he exclaimed, leaning forward as if to touch his shoulder, even though the table was too wide for him to do so. "Everything's an exchange, you know. And before you say something like"—he lifted his shoulders and straightened an invisible long collar like a G-Man from a 1940's movie—"'I could make it tough on you if you don't cooperate, see,' I'll have you know that you've caught 18 is 9 at one of its cleanest moments. I never have anything illegal on premises before the big New Year's party because I know the predilections of law enforcement."

Wilson considered pushing anyway but backed off. "What are you fishing for, Aloysius?"

He lowered his voice and looked left to right. "I'd like to read *Die Geheimnisse der Vögel*, but I'd need the translated version."

"What? Your German not up to snuff?" Wilson taunted.

"Not all of us have access to the two best occult minds in the world on a daily basis, Agent Wilson," he pouted, obliquely referring to the twins.

"Chloe and Dot shoot you down again?" Wilson enjoyed goading him a little too much.

"I just don't get how they think!" he burst out, honestly wounded by the barb. Aloysius had tried many times to befriend the pair, but they were utterly uninterested. For the briefest moment, Wilson felt sorry for him. To not be liked was a deep cut for someone so gregarious.

Die Geheimnisse der Vögel was a treatise written in 1687 by Albert the Fifth, Duke of Saxe-Coburg. It was a rambling magical codex with many false leads, but it contained two remarkable magics. The first was a spell for conversing with birds, and the second was a spell that allowed birds to understand human tongues. Lady Jane Franklin translated it into English in 1853 in her quest to use the powers of the book in her search for her missing husband; even though she knew some German, she found the original spells less effective than the ones translated into her native tongue. It didn't take a leap of imagination to figure out why Aloysius was so interested—being able to turn birds into spies provided all sorts of interesting opportunities.

"How about this," Wilson offered. "I'll talk to them and ask for you…unlike you, I *do* get how they think." Wilson made a mental note to remind the twins he had spared them Aloysius-exposure the next time he needed a favor or Dot was in a bit of pique.

Aloysius leaned forward against the table in excitement. "Do you think you could get it? Would that work?"

Wilson flipped a hand in a gesture of *que sera, sera*. "I can't promise anything, but they do like me."

"Done!" Aloysius held out his hand.

Wilson waited a second before sealing the deal with a firm shake; it was best to let the club owner think he'd won a hard concession. Wilson knew full well that the real English version of *Die Geheimnisse der Vögel* would never end up in Aloysius's hands. If the librarians were feeling generous, the best he would get is the faux translation the Mine produced years ago for one of its operations in East Berlin, which had all the powerful parts excised and replaced with linguistically similar passages lacking power. Wilson always thought the Cold War history of the Salt Mine would make a remarkable documentary, if only it wasn't an organization that officially didn't exist.

Aloysius was still beaming from the semblance of success Wilson had granted him, and he knew to strike while the iron was hot. "I need information on any Dionysian activities you know of," Wilson plied him for information, "preferably anything recent…the past three to six months."

Aloysius tilted his head in puzzlement. "Dionysian? As in Dionysius?"

"Yes, that would be what I'm looking for," Wilson confirmed.

"What a strange thing to ask for," he muttered. "I haven't heard anything Dionysius-related, other than the normal parties dedicated to him."

"No recent changes or upticks? Any new movers?" Wilson persisted.

"Well, there's the big party tonight, and that's happening all the world over," Aloysius struggled to find something useful.

"Yes, I'm aware that people party on New Year's Eve," Wilson dryly replied.

Couldn't tell from your dress or demeanor, Aloysius sassed back in his head, but he held his tongue—he really wanted his book. Instead, he held up his hands and shrugged his shoulders. "I could make something up, but that would just waste your time and piss you off. I haven't heard of anything Dionysian that's in any way unusual. Sorry."

Chapter Eighteen

Detroit, Michigan, USA
1st of January, 11:50 a.m. (GMT-5)

Martinez christened the new year with three lucky tamales—usually for lunch, because who starts New Year's Day with breakfast? It was something her family always did when she was growing up, and she'd decided to continue the practice after a lapse of a few years in college.

Finding New Year's Day tamales was easily accomplished in Portland, where the weather was mild and she knew the city, but it was proving more difficult in Detroit. Solidly below freezing with thick fat snowflakes falling, she'd already gone to two places just to find one closed permanently and the other with a handwritten "Family Emergency" note on the front door. She parked in their lot and dug around on her phone, determined to hold with tradition despite the foreign terrain.

Her persistence paid off, and she finally found a location that answered her call. It was a cash-only place adjacent to a warehouse district, and the reviews describing it as "humble" were being generous, but it hit the spot. It was the kind of place that made its own horchata and had a crockpot of home-pickled jalapeños beside its salsa bar.

As she dug into the last of her tamales, the Spanish weather report ended and the business news hour started. The lead story was the surprise resignation of Charles Roberts, founder and CEO of Detrop Pharmaceuticals, due to a terminal illness. The CEO wasn't expected to live out the month, and he was being replaced by another founder, Emily Thibodeaux, the current COO. The anchor made a brief comment on Roberts's legacy of philanthropy through the repeated release of drug patents, making his groundbreaking medications more affordable to people all around the globe. Martinez scarfed down the last tamale and checked the business news sites online. After five minutes, she called Wilson's mobile.

He picked up on the fourth ring. "This is Wilson."

"Have you heard the news about Detrop Pharmaceuticals?"

"No," he answered in a curt but polite tone. Martinez could hear voices in the background, and he was more terse than normal. *He's not able to speak freely*, she surmised.

"The CEO just resigned due to terminal illness."

"What kind?"

"They didn't say and none of the information I can find online says, either. Also, he's known for great acts of philanthropy," she added suggestively. "I think we should check it out."

"Agreed. Hold on a second." She waited a brief moment, and then he returned. "Sorry about that, couldn't talk. This can't be a coincidence. I'll notify Leader. I suggest you get packed again. Where's Detrop Pharmaceuticals located, and where can we find its CEO?"

"Cambridge, Mass; CEO lives in a brownstone in Boston."

"At least it will be a short flight," he commented before hanging up.

Martinez looked up to the television, but commercials were now playing. She decided on a fourth tamale for extra luck before going back to her hotel.

*****

Wilson slid his phone back into his pocket and returned to the living room of his old house in Corktown—his abode prior to building the 500. "My apologies," he addressed the two young men inside. "I had to take that. So you're wanting out of your lease?"

"We hate to ask, but we can't take it anymore," the taller of the two flanneled and bearded early-twenty-year-olds responded. Wilson did not understand the lumberjack look.

"Have you been doing what I suggested? Leaving all the doors open? Not going into the basement or the attic?" Wilson prompted.

They heartily nodded, and the taller continued, "We've done that, and they still keep slamming them shut. We even put felt protectors—the kind for chair and table legs—along the door jams to soften the sounds, but they're doing it throughout the night."

The smaller of the pair chimed in, "I know you said the place was haunted before we signed the agreement, but man, I didn't really believe in stuff like that. I thought you were just being weird." He squirmed uncomfortably. "A few bumps and noises at night that I can cover up with earplugs is one thing, but this…I can't take any more of this. It's scaring the shit out of me."

"It's okay, they don't hurt anyone," Wilson explained, "but I understand what you're saying. I'll make you guys an offer: you won't have to pay rent this month, but you'll have to stay another week and see if I can get them to calm down. If I can't, we'll break the lease, and you can leave whenever you want. I don't want you two living somewhere you don't feel safe."

They looked at each other and had a silent conversation between facial expressions and nods—a month's free rent was a sweet deal. They both agreed.

"Good," Wilson praised them for their sensibility. "It sounds like I have some last-minute unexpected travel for work, but it shouldn't be more than a day or two. Once I'm back, we'll set up a time for me to come over and placate our restless guests. In the meantime, take these." He handed them each a silk sachet. "Place it over the threshold of your bedroom door. This will keep Millie and Wolfhard out of your bedroom while you sleep."

They accepted the parcels, skeptically examining them. "Millie and Wolfhard?" the smaller questioned.

"That's the ghosts' names. There's a third one, but she never says anything," Wilson explained. "Now, whatever you do, don't break the seal on the sachets, and know this—once you put them up, the ghosts are going to get more rambunctious because you've just made part of their house off limits to them. They're not going to like it, and they *will* make their displeasure known."

"That sounds threatening," the larger tenant commented.

"It will seem so, but remember, they're all bluster. They can't really hurt you."

"Couldn't they like, throw knives at us or something like that?" the smaller worried.

Wilson gave the kid a reassuring smile, but it was all teeth and no eyes. "That's not a possibility here. They were Quakers and committed to peace. They were killed because they chose to not defend themselves, and they aren't going to start resorting to violence now."

That seemed to calm them down. *How bad could Quaker ghosts be?* the taller one reasoned in his head to justify staying in the house for a month of free rent. Wilson left his tenants and made his way back to the 500, and as he drove away, the smaller one muttered under his breath, "Oh man, that guy is *really* weird." The other said nothing, but nodded slowly, his thick beard moving up and down over his plaid shirt.

Chapter Nineteen

Boston, Massachusetts, USA
1st of January, 9:40 p.m. (GMT-5)

"Dionysus, as in the bacchanal Dionysus?" Martinez puzzled. "Does he even count as a god anymore? I thought he was just an excuse for college students to throw toga parties."

"For where two or three gather in my name…" Wilson alluded to Christian scripture as he navigated the slick streets of Boston in their rental car. "He is also the god of wine, and last time I looked, there is plenty of that going around."

"So what's the plan when we get there?" Martinez inquired. She had reviewed Roberts's hastily prepared file along with the history of Detrop Pharmaceuticals.

"Our first priority is figuring out if Roberts is even involved, and if he is, determining if he's our magician or another victim," Wilson replied as he shifted gears.

"And how are we going to do that?"

"Divide and conquer. You distract him with generic softball questions while I disperse the salt and wait for a pattern. If we have the same distribution that we saw at Grollo's home, he's a victim. If a very different pattern emerges, one associated with

Dionysus, then we have our magician and we have to neutralize him from doing any more damage, even if karma has caught up with him."

"And if there is nothing?"

An irritated look came over Wilson's face. "That's trickier. Either he's one hell of a coincidence or he's been scrubbed and there is no way of distinguishing if he is the perpetrator or victim. Just be ready to follow my lead once I have some answers."

Martinez carefully loaded the salt into the ivory tube, taking care to hold it upright as Wilson slowed down and parallel parked down the street from Roberts's home. She passed it to Wilson before they exited their vehicle.

The doorbell angered Jane Bennet. Ms. Thibodeaux and Mr. Phillips had already told everyone who'd called that Mr. Roberts was not accepting visitors, and she was certain that the only reason the bell was ringing was that some fool believed that the rules didn't apply to them. As she went down two flights of stairs, she managed not to stomp until the very last few steps, when she could no longer contain her fuming any longer. She flicked on the exterior light and saw two people through the peephole—a small man and a tall, broad-shouldered woman.

"Go away! We're not accepting visitors," she stage whispered through the door, trying to stay as quiet as possible to avoid disturbing Mr. Roberts.

The small man held up a wallet. "I'm Special Agent Wilson

and this is Special Agent Martinez, from the FBI. We're here to speak with Mr. Charles Roberts."

This threw the nurse for a loop. She'd never encountered a real FBI agent, and now there were two of them. She wasn't quite sure what to do, so she cracked open the door and told them to wait until she talked with Mr. Roberts.

Wilson and Martinez patiently stood in the cold outside until the door opened again; this time they were welcomed into the expansive brownstone. "Thank you for waiting. I'm Jane Bennet, Mr. Roberts's nurse. Let's get your jackets into the closet, shall we?" she greeted them. Martinez smiled at the familiar tenor of the request-that-is-really-an-order; her mother had been a nurse and she had heard it many times while growing up.

"I don't know why you're here—and that's not my business—but I expect you have something important that needs doing. However, I want to caution you that Mr. Roberts is in a bad way. Try not to exhaust him if you can; he doesn't have a lot of time left and I'd like to make the time he does have as good as possible," she spoke softly, leading them up to the third floor.

The hospital bed seemed to engulf the frail frame of Charles Roberts. An IV bag hung on a rack, slowing dripping into his left arm. Neither agent had ever seen anyone in his condition outside of WWII documentaries; he was so thin that Martinez hardly recognized him from the pictures in his file. Thanks to their training, they did not show their shock upon entry.

"Mr. Roberts, this is Agent Wilson and Agent Martinez, from the FBI," Ms. Bennet introduced the pair. "I'll be in the next room with the door closed; just ring me when they're ready to leave." As she was closing the door, she flashed a warning look to the agents and tapped on her watch.

Once they were alone, Roberts spoke up, rasping like dry leaves in a cold autumn wind, "My apologies for Jane, she's the protective sort. She believes that sparing me effort has some value this late in the game." He weakly waved them closer. "Take a seat. From your faces, it looks like you've something important to discuss with me, and honestly, this may be the only chance you get—better make it worth your while."

There was a pair of matched plush chairs, one on either side of his hulking bed. Wilson moved to take the chair on the far side while Martinez took the well-worn seat normally inhabited by his nurse. "So, to what do I owe the pleasure of not just one, but two FBI agents arriving unannounced well after dinnertime?" he asked.

"Our apologies, Mr. Roberts, but once we'd heard of your deteriorating condition, we thought it imprudent to wait." Martinez drew his attention as Wilson bent low and blew out the salt in the guise of moving his chair closer to the bed. "I don't want to appear too forward, but do you mind telling us what exactly you're dying from?"

Roberts was taken aback at her candid question. "It's

refreshing to speak with someone who doesn't feel the need euphemize death, Agent Martinez. Yes, I'm dying…I'm just trying to hold out 'til my birthday out of stubbornness. From what? That's the big mystery. No one knows." His initial enthusiasm petered out as he spoke until he was at nearly half his normal speaking speed by the end. Wilson watched the salt scatter on the ground in front of his feet. He kept his face impassive as he waited.

"Surely someone must know," Martinez pressed.

"You'd think so, wouldn't you? And don't call me Shirley," he joked, wracking himself into a mix of laughter and coughing. "Sorry, I've got to get in as many of the classics as I can before I shuffle off this mortal coil. But yes, Agent Martinez, healthy people—like I was until recently—just don't waste away, and I'm much too young for geriatric failure to thrive." The coughing fit fully took him. He motioned for the cup of water by Martinez, and she stood, assisting the straw into his mouth. She flashed a look to Wilson—he subtly shook his head side to side, indicating that nothing had happened yet.

Roberts gathered himself and started talking again. "They ran every test they could think of, and nothing came up positive. So here I am. My best case scenario is that they'll figure out what's happening to me after I'm dead, and then I'll have a new condition or disease named after me. Roberts's Disease: when you stop being able to digest and just waste away." The salt began to quiver and shift on the hardwood floor.

"When did your sickness begin?" Martinez continued her questioning, buying Wilson more time. She could see him glance down out of her periphery.

Roberts hesitated before answering, "I first started noticing it in late October. But enough about my problems…why have you come here? What can I do for you?"

Wilson watched the grains of salt coalesce into a familiar pattern—the same as in Grollo's calligraphy drawer. He finally raised his eyes from the floor and gave Martinez a barely perceptible nod. Wilson swiped his foot across the pattern, should anyone be looking remotely for signs of their investigation, before interjecting, "I don't know if you're aware, but there have been five deaths in the past two to three months. All CEOs of pharmaceutical companies, like yourself."

"Former CEO," Roberts corrected. "I'm retired now. But no, I wasn't aware. You think they're connected somehow and that I'm going to be the next victim?" He had another coughing fit, but it felt contrived to Wilson. *Was he buying himself time to think?* he wondered.

"There doesn't seem to be any connection between the deceased that we can see. The first death was a heroin overdose—"

"You don't have to own a pharmaceutical company to get your hands on that," Roberts quipped.

Wilson agreed and continued, "The second was found dead in the Ganges—there wasn't a listed reason for the death, and the body was cremated before we had a chance to investigate. The third death was Carlos Segovia, who died from a car wreck during an illegal street race in Barcelona."

"What?! Carlos is dead? I hadn't heard about that."

"You knew Mr. Segovia?" Martinez jumped on the first personal connection they had encountered—two of the victims knew each other.

"We'd met a few times at various conventions and really hit it off. I've always been a fan of Formula One racing, and he was nearly obsessed with it, so we got together and shot the shit whenever we had the time. Last I saw him was when I was trying to convince some of my fellow CEOs at the smaller drug companies to relinquish some of their patents."

Wilson pounced, "When and where was that?"

"Sometime in mid-October; the fifteenth, if I'm remembering properly. I'm not sure…you'd have to check with Emily."

"Emily Thibodaux, the new CEO, former COO?" Martinez confirmed.

"And one of my oldest friends, yes." He paused for another drink before stating, "None of these seem to have anything to do with me."

"The fourth death was Simon Collins, CEO of Ire Laboratories. He was murdered by a prostitute," Wilson responded.

"That can only be coincidence, then. It's absolutely nothing related to my condition."

"Mr. Collins was killed because he started to eat the prostitute he'd hired," Wilson disclosed.

"Eat?" Roberts coughed out, eyes wide as he was forced to take a bit more water. His voice grinding out of his throat like sandpaper on stone, he repeated, "He tried to eat her? Alive?"

Wilson nodded. "She killed him when she kicked to defend herself—he bit the inside of her thigh—and her stiletto went through his eye and into the brain. When they investigated his house, they found the partially eaten corpses of two missing prostitutes."

"That's just horrible! I would have never suspected that about him." Roberts seemed genuinely shocked.

"You knew Mr. Collins as well?" Martinez probed.

"Yes. I wouldn't be surprised if I knew all of the people on your list. Part of this business is being aware of your competitors. Collins's behavior strikes me as particularly strange, as he'd just agreed to open a patent on an HPV vaccine he had…not what you'd expect from a man with an obvious hatred of women."

"A person's face is rarely the self," Wilson responded obliquely, "but this behavior seemed to be out of character for Mr. Collins. He had a long history of availing himself of the services of prostitutes, but the prior ones that we tracked down never mentioned any tendency toward aggression or dominance, let alone actual violence."

"Did you know a Carlmon Grollo of Brockham

Laboratories?" Martinez went to the next name on the list.

Roberts weakly nodded. "Now that one, I heard about. Supposedly some sort of suicide?"

"The ME's report listed suicide, yes," Wilson responded, carefully assessing Roberts's haggard face. "But there's more to it. This is all confidential and should not be shared, but given the circumstances, I feel that you should know."

"Dead men tell no tales, huh, Agent Wilson?" For the briefest moment, Martinez saw a light in his sunken eyes and a hint of the man featured on all those magazine covers she'd skimmed on the flight from Detroit.

"Precisely, Mr. Roberts, but that isn't my main motivation." Wilson made eye contact with the dying man. "To be frank, I think there's something strange going on here, that these deaths are related, but I cannot for the life of me put them together. As you are still alive, I'm hoping you can help me find the pieces I'm missing from this puzzle."

Roberts briefly struggled into a more-upright position, his interest piqued. Wilson waited until he was settled before continuing, "Mr. Grollo asphyxiated while eating. This is not unusual, but what he was eating is very unusual. He asphyxiated while eating one of his favorite paintings, the eighth he had consumed that night. He died from eating William Holman Hunt's *Ophelia*." Both agents expected a reaction, but were unprepared for what happened—instead of shock or horror, Mr. Roberts started to silently cry.

"Are you okay?" Martinez asked, reaching out to touch the edge of his bed.

"No, Agent Martinez, I am decidedly not okay," he responded quietly, looking back and forth between the agents' faces. "Can I ask you a favor?"

"Sure," Martinez answered.

"I have something I want to tell you, but I don't want anyone to know about it. Can I trust you with something… something terrible?"

"Absolutely," she responded before Wilson could say anything otherwise.

"I don't know what I'm dying from, but I think I know what's killing me. I can't eat anything. I can't hold any food down without throwing up." A minor mania fell over him; the pace of his words hastened instead of slowing down, and his face fully animated. "All I can think about now, constantly going round and round in my brain, trying to override my will, is money. Money is the only thing I want to eat now. It gets me higher than a kite and makes me feel better than I've ever felt before." His shoulders twitched.

"When did this begin?" Wilson calmly inquired.

"October 29th was the first time. I was nervous, edgy, and fiddling with my wallet for some reason when the bills kept calling to me. Without thinking, I took one out and started eating it. It made me feel wonderful, and I ate my way through everything I had in one sitting. Once I regained my senses and the horror set in, I pretended it didn't happen, that it was just a one-time thing.

"And then I found myself in front of an ATM on my way home, salivating. It happened daily, until I realized that eating money might kill me—I couldn't find any information on what type of ink is used and I didn't know if it was toxic. But that's not surprising, right? You wouldn't want that information easily available to counterfeiters. It was then that I switched to pure gold coins. Gold's non-toxic and I could eat as much as I needed without hurting myself…well, within reason, of course.

"I went on that way for a while, but eventually my body stopped wanting any real food. First the smell bothered me, and then the taste, and finally I couldn't keep anything down and just stopped eating. Except for gold…gold was always perfect." Roberts's face softened just talking about his obsession.

The agents exchanged glances, and she noted the flare of Wilson's nostrils and the intent focus in his eyes. "What's your prior relationship with money? Have you ever had this craving before?" he followed up.

"I've never…wait…what were the names of the other dead?"

"The other victims?"

"Yes, the ones before Carlos."

"Adam Vogler and Mithun Chand," Wilson recited from memory.

Roberts burst into another coughing fit that brought in his nurse, who gave Wilson and Martinez a cross look, but she left again once everything was under control. After taking several sips of water, Roberts continued, "Yes, I knew them all. In fact, they were guests…" He suddenly took a deep breath, his emaciated chest expanding dramatically, and blurted out, "They were all in a meeting I arranged to try and schmooze more companies to release their patents. We were all there!"

*****

Roberts's nurse nearly slammed the door behind them, but her furious face barely registered to Wilson and Martinez. "Finally!" Martinez burst out. "We have a solid connection!"

"That we do," Wilson chirped and almost smiled. "As soon as we get the Mine working on this, we'll sniff out the trail of the bastard responsible." They hustled to their car. "First, we'll go to Detrop's headquarters—I'll drive if you make the calls. If there's a chance to save Mr. Roberts's life, we need to act fast. Press the COO and CFO as much as necessary to get them to meet us tonight; if they're as good of friends as he claims, it shouldn't take much."

Martinez nodded and started calling while Wilson slowly drove toward the Charles River; the weather had taken a turn for the worse during their conversation. Roberts faded quickly after putting together the connection, but not before giving them the private numbers for both the COO and the CFO of Detrop Pharmaceuticals, with reassurances that they would be able to get the information the agents wanted.

As Martinez made the calls, Wilson could hear the concern from the other side of the line. She didn't need to do much convincing—the fact that Roberts had given them the number was enough for both to drop whatever they were doing and head to their office. That boded well, in Wilson's opinion.

The agents pulled up to the building's parking garage, but without a pass card, they had to wait until Thibodaux arrived to follow her in. Phillips arrived seconds later, parking next to them just as they were exiting their cars.

"Ms. Thibodaux, Mr. Phillips, thank you for agreeing to meet with us on such short notice, and my apologies for interrupting you at such a late hour. I am Agent Wilson and this is Agent Martinez of the FBI—"

Thibodaux cut him short, "You think you know what's killing Chuck?"

"We're not sure of the precise mechanism, but all the CEOs who attended the London meeting last October, wherein Mr. Roberts tried to convince them to release patents into the public domain, are now dead, Mr. Roberts excluded."

"Poison?!" Phillips exclaimed. "You think they were poisoned?"

"We're not sure about that yet, but that's what we're going to be investigating," Martinez replied. "What we need is all the information on the meeting you can provide us—particularly regarding ancillary staffing and companies employed during the meeting. We would like to know the names of every person who had access to all of the CEOs. Mr. Roberts said that you two could provide that information."

"I have most of that on my computer," Phillips verified their assertion, leading the way to the elevators. "You have the information on the samples factory, right Emily?"

"I do," Thibodaux confirmed. Seeing the quizzical looks of the agents, she explained, "Chuck took samples of the meds he released into the public domain from our favored manufacturer. He wanted to show them how the branding on the boxes would prominently mention their company names, informing customers that these medicines are available at a much lower cost because their companies are committed to providing the best healthcare possible."

"The marketing guys call it 'meaningful advertising,' but Chuck just viewed it as a deal-sweetener to convince them to go along," Phillips added, unlocking the door to his office. "Here we are; let me get everything booted and we'll be good to go."

"How many people were at the meeting?" Thibodaux asked as they waited.

"Six, including Mr. Roberts," Wilson answered.

"And the other five are all dead?"

Wilson nodded. "The last one died from eating unusual

objects—choked to death." Thibodaux and Phillips exchanged intense glances at this information but said nothing—they'd made a promise to Chuck. Their looks didn't pass unnoticed by Agents Wilson and Martinez, who had made promises of their own. The desktop seemed to take forever to boot as the two pairs of people bound by their word waited in stifled silence. The chime of the finished boot sounded as familiar icons flashed on the screen.

"Here we go!" Phillips broke the tense quiet. "This folder has all the information about the meeting. Where do you want me to send it?"

Chapter Twenty

Boston, Massachusetts, USA
2nd of January, 6:00 a.m. (GMT-5)

Martinez woke to an unexpected knock on her hotel room door. "Who is it?" she groggily called out.

"It's me," Wilson's flat voice responded. "You need to get up and get packed. We've got to catch a flight to London in two hours. I brought donuts." Martinez peered at the clock and cursed the early hour. She hadn't gotten much sleep, pouring over the files for "A Generous Hand"—Roberts's initiative to persuade companies to release patents—in search of any additional connections between the group of victims. While nothing immediately stood out, she couldn't shake the feeling that she was missing something. She'd only given up her search a few hours ago, not expecting Wilson to bang on her door before sunrise.

"Gimme a second," she yelled as she threw some clothes on and pulled her hair into a hasty knot before opening the door.

Wilson stood in the door wearing a crisp suit and carrying a paper plate upon which rested three donuts. "I didn't know what you liked, so I got an assortment." He handed her the plate. "I'll meet you in the lobby in ten minutes."

Martinez inhaled the first donut while she quickly pulled herself together, combing her hair and changing into work clothes in front of the mirror. She could always touch up her light makeup on the plane, but she was pretty sure Wilson would object to her rolling into the airport in her PJs. She then gathered her things, taking care to pack the top in alignment with the luggage lining's profile. *Can't say this new choice of career isn't exciting*, she thought as she started on the second donut, a blueberry cake that was a little on the stodgy side. *They weren't kidding when they said to always keep your passport on you.*

After a bite of raspberry jelly donut—she dared not risk the powdered sugar or the red filling on the run—Martinez did a final scan of her room to make sure she didn't leave anything before joining Wilson downstairs, looking up from a watch check. They nodded to each other and fell into step toward the rental car. Wilson was already navigating the light pre-rush hour traffic to Logan International before Martinez quizzed him. "I take it you've figured something out?"

"I was up most of the night poring through the "A Generous Hand" files before I finally gave up and called Chloe and Dot. They spotted what was niggling at me immediately," Wilson confessed with a hint of disgust. "If time wasn't so crucial, we would have eventually caught it—the catering company for the meeting is owned by the cousin of the coroner that was at the scene of the last death."

"So we're off to interview him with DCI Jones?"

"That would be my inclination if this were a mundane investigation, but the use of magic complicates matters. The closer we get to the source, the more dangerous it becomes—not just to us, but to everyone associated with us. This time is pure espionage.

"We're switching aliases. Our cover story is that we're a couple visiting the UK for pleasure. Pick out one or two things you want to see in London, so you have something to chat about in case customs is nosier than normal. Let me know what they are so I can look them up and have something to add to the conversation if need be. Focus on places for a spring wedding," Wilson briefed her before pulling out a small jewelry box from his inner jacket pocket and depositing it in Martinez's lap.

The well-worn hinge creaked as she opened the box, revealing a two-carat princess-cut diamond solitaire set in a white gold band. "Wilson, we just met. This is happening all so fast!" she teased him as she plucked the ring from its cushioned slit. "Wait, is this magic? Am I going to get hit with karmic debt if I put it on?"

The corners of Wilson's mouth twitched. "Nothing magical, just the crushing weight of impending matrimony."

Martinez slipped the ring on her left hand. "How did you know my size? And have you been carrying this thing with you the whole time?"

"I didn't, Leader did, and yes, I come prepared," he answered, coasting onto the exit ramp for rental car returns. "I've got the Mine working on pulling up information on both the coroner and the caterer while we work our way across the Atlantic—we should have something by the time we land. I've booked us a room at a B&B in Uxbridge, which isn't far from where we need to be but outside the boundaries for the Thames Valley Police Force where DCI Jones is posted. It's highly unlikely that we'd pop up on his radar, but being outside his force's jurisdiction should help on that front."

Wilson and Martinez did the travel dance—return rental car, check in luggage, security, boarding—only to do it again once the plane touched down—deplane, gather luggage, go through customs, acquire rental car. While Martinez wasn't a stranger to air travel, she lacked the ease of movement Wilson had mastered over countless trips. An old war-horse of a traveler, he weaved through gates and terminals with cold efficiency, scarcely affected by changes in location and time. They checked into their room, unpacked their luggage, and tore into the take-out Martinez insisted they get before they were in for the night. The wafting scent of curry awakened her stomach, which had only nibbled since her breakfast of donuts. Now comfortably in her PJs, she unearthed her dish and naan before handing the bag to Wilson.

They ate in silence, glued to their phones reading the files from the Mine. The first file was concerning the coroner Cyril Basil Hicks, age fifty-seven, born in London, educated at Eton, then the University of Birmingham in law with business studies. Hicks descended from a once-influential Buckinghamshire family that lost all their possessions during the troubled years of the Great Depression. Currently practicing law in a private practice in High Wycombe, where he also acted as coroner for the Chiltern Hills (aka Chilterns) rural communities.

"He's Eton," Martinez blurted out. "Grollo was Eton as well, and only a year older. There's a decent chance they knew each other from school."

"Good catch," Wilson said. "I'm not an expert regarding education in the UK, but isn't Eton one of their upper-class schools?"

"That's an understatement, if my BBC habit is to be trusted," Martinez replied, quickly looking up Eton on the net to confirm. "Yes, it's a very influential school. Apparently nineteen prime ministers have come from it, along with dozens of other culturally-influential people."

"I'm assuming it's expensive; the Hicks family must have done some horse trading to get him into Eton if they lost the bulk of their wealth before WWII."

"Probably not an unreasonable assumption. Eton is just south of Slough; it's nearby, if we need to access it for some reason," she responded. "And note that his son is *not* attending his father's alma mater." Martinez played with the remains of her curry. "How very un-British."

"Even legacies have to pay their tuition bills..." Wilson stated wryly. "Well, if Hicks and Grollo didn't know each other at school, they certainly knew each other later in life," he mentioned after a cursory glance over an interview Grollo had given to a financial magazine. "Hicks was one of the original investors in Brockham Laboratories."

One of Martinez's eyebrows raised as she scrolled through the rest of the file. "Nothing more concrete on his financials?" she voiced, a little disappointed.

"That will take a little more time." Wilson flipped a little further. "Public records show the purchase of his country home shortly after the company went public, at a not insignificant sum."

It felt obscene to say out loud, but Martinez whistled in appreciation when she found the page Wilson was browsing. She shook her head in dismay. "It's all in who you know."

"Apparently. Although it didn't really help Grollo," Wilson commented before moving on and skimming the file on the catering company. Bliss Catering, founded in 1998, owned by Felicia Pemberton, cousin of Cyril Hicks. Bliss was headquartered in Wembley, a part of northeast London, with an income of a quarter million pounds per year and four employees. "Ah, the caterer is a small operation," he observed. "That'll make this much easier."

Martinez pulled up a browser and searched for Bliss

Catering, finding their website and social media presence. Her hunger now sated, she swiped through the pictures of confections, artfully plated meals, and buffets. "Looks like they mostly do weddings, birthday and anniversary parties, bar mitzvahs, those sorts of things." She kept flipping until her eyes gleamed. "Hello, look what we have here."

Wilson looked up from the couch—his bed for the night. "What?"

"One of their signature cakes—the 24 Karat Cake, a carrot cake covered with real gold." Martinez rose from the bed and turned her phone around for Wilson. He turned his gaze to a picture of an edible gold brick faux-stamped with a seal declaring it "24 Carrot."

Wilson wasn't a man who believed in coincidences. "Let's start with the catering company first thing tomorrow before hitting the coroner. It'll be easy to get close enough to them to do some salt detection as we did with Mr. Roberts." He fluffed his pillow before turning back to his reading.

Chapter Twenty-One

Piddington, Buckinghamshire, UK
3rd of January, 3:55 a.m. (GMT)

All his life, Cyril Hicks wanted power. It was his birthright, ripped out from beneath him by the mistakes of his father and his father's father. Perhaps even further back. He didn't know how far the poor stewardship went, but the fact was the life he was supposed to have—the life he was bred for—was an unkept promise.

Of course, as a young child he didn't know any better. The subtle jabs his parents endured from their friends, their elaborate schemes to project wealth beyond their means, and the white lies they told to save face were simply the way it was. It wasn't until he was shipped off to school that he truly understood his precarious social position.

It started innocently enough, back in his Eton days. He was little more than a frightened, sniveling thirteen-year-old boy, separated from his parents and boyhood friends and thrust into a world to which his family no longer belonged. It was an honor to be invited into the Double Face Society, a group of lads who practiced the "dark arts." They would sneak around, meet in secret locations at special times, and perform spells and rituals in their learned Greek and Latin. Many a division master was hexed, as well as swaths of the Eton student body, but nothing bad ever really happened.

Most members of the Double Face Society strayed from the arts after graduation. For them, it was just a bit of fun, but things were different for Hicks. He continued his study of ancient occult books, and he took his knowledge into the wider world of the occult, eventually becoming a practitioner of Chaos Magick. Again, nothing happened, but it gave him solace from the daily grind his life had become after school—trapped in a dry world of law, and a loveless marriage that produced one son he was all too happy to ship off once he came of age. Although, not to Eton...they couldn't afford Eton.

Hicks thought his luck had finally changed when Carlmon Grollo, one of his old Double Face chums, hit it big in pharmaceuticals. Hicks became a multimillionaire overnight when the IPO took place. He took great pleasure in reminding his grasping wife of the row she'd put him through when she'd discovered he'd sank their life savings into Brockham Laboratories as one of its first investors. Oh, how she delighted in reminding him that she owned half.

For a few years, things were good...at least, as good as they'd ever been for him. There was more of everything: nicer clothes, bigger house, fine dining, shopping, parties, and swaths of well-connected friends. He even started collecting for the pleasure of owning rare and precious things.

His shining acquisition was an extremely rare coin obtained through black market connections he'd made during one of his many trips to Monte Carlo. The ancient Greek gold coin was minted in Phokaia and featured the head of King Midas. There were only six in the world, and he had one of them. The price was exorbitant and there was no doubt it was stolen, but once he saw it, he knew he had to have it.

For a long time, he'd assumed wealth was power, but the more he spent, the more he realized how hollow it was, and he paid dearly for that lesson. By that time, however, he'd already purchased the expensive country house and put the boy into a better school. His wife had grown accustomed to having money to spend, and he had acquired a taste for the finer things in life.

The increasingly frequent trips to casinos and a series of beautiful-but-expensive women did their part to drain the coffers as well. He'd had to pay more than a few of them handsomely for their discretion—he would rather be penniless than give his wife legal fuel for a divorce. To keep up appearances, he started borrowing against the value of his holdings in Brockham Laboratories, freeing up capital for his appetites while holding on to what he owned. Having money to burn was better than not, even if it didn't quench his thirst.

Like many men of a certain age do, he revisited the things of his youth—things that he'd enjoyed when life was simpler. Nostalgia was a strong drug, and he found himself drawn back into the old ways he'd learned at Eton: the pentagrams and circles used in blood rites, and invocations read from ancient leather-bound books.

The first time he'd summoned a demon, he was as surprised as it. After nearly four and a half decades, one of his rituals had actually worked. It wasn't powerful—little more than a glorified imp—but it was enough to send Hicks screaming in fear from the loft over his garage. It took him more than an hour to summon the courage to return. When Hicks found the fiend bound as intended, he was filled with something he'd rarely experienced before: a feeling of power. It was better than anything money had bought him.

And then his world came crumbling down. One night over dinner with his old Eton chum, he'd learned that Grollo was thinking about releasing several medication patents into the public domain, cutting the profitability of Brockham Laboratories by nearly thirty percent. He was even having a meeting in London with a handful of other CEOs considering similar action.

Hicks flew into a panic. Investors were a skittish bunch and markets got nervous when companies even talked about reduced profits, regardless of the reason. If Brockham Laboratories' stock price dropped more than fifty percent overnight—which was a serious possibility—his loans would be called. The cascade of financial and social ruin that would follow was unthinkable.

Without giving away how dire his position was, he begged

Grollo to consider the impact on the investors, but Hicks knew it wasn't his decision to make. The rug was about to be pulled out from under him and he was powerless to stop it...which made him turn to something that did make him feel powerful. Had he been a more experienced practitioner, he would have known it was a bad idea to talk to demons, much less take their counsel. They were chaos and evil and lies wrapped in a seductive skin. But to Hicks, it was someone he had power over. It was someone to pour out all the disappointments and bitter anger that filled his entire life. Under the demon's sway, Hicks came to see that Grollo was trying to ruin him and needed to be taken care of. All of them needed to be taken care of.

It was a simple plan, which appealed to Hicks. The demon promised his school chum wouldn't get hurt; it would only make him and the other CEOs lust for money and ensure no patents would be released. Lulled by the demon's empty promises and pretty words, Hicks relented. Had Hicks been more knowledgeable in the arts, he would have known the worth of a demon's oath.

Hicks followed its instructions to the letter and met his old friend again, this time affecting support. "What's a few pounds here or there to people like us? As Etonians, we have an obligation to the people," Hicks had said. He even offered to have his cousin cater the upcoming event. Hicks had Grollo in the palm of his hand for just the price of some excellent port and cigars. It was all too easy; men like Grollo were used to everyone applauding them and bending over backward to help.

Hicks loathed to put his precious Midas Coin to the file, but the demon assured him it was the only way. By grinding it down to a powder, it could easily be dusted over his cousin's signature dessert with none the wiser. Once eaten, it would amplify the desires of the consumer. None of the CEOs in attendance would be releasing any patents then, because what all wealthy men desired more than anything else was more wealth, didn't they?

When everything went as planned and there was no more talk of reducing profits from Grollo, Hicks was thrilled beyond measure. The rush of success overcame his remorse at sacrificing half of his wonderful coin, and he still had the other half to cherish, although it took some time before he could bring himself to look at it in its defaced state. When he did finally summon up the resolve to visit its display case, he found it whole again. He couldn't believe his luck. He had gotten away with everything, even his treasured coin—his beautiful, whole, gleaming coin.

If Hicks had stopped there, everything might have been fine. But like all gamblers, he had a problem walking away from the table when he was ahead. He started keeping the Midas Coin with him at all times for good luck, thinking it safe because he'd never ingested any of it. But its near proximity only amplified his desire, not for wealth, but for power—his true obsession.

Like a poker player on tilt, he upped the ante. He furiously dove into his books again, looking for a greater fiend to summon. The prospect of more power was too tempting. So consumed was he that he was unfazed by the unusual death of his one-time chum. Eventually, Hicks set his sights on summoning Buer, bestower of powerful familiars—to bind such a demon to himself would exponentially increase his power.

His spell worked, thanks to the power in the Midas Coin, but his grasp exceeded his skill and he was snared. That was why the twisted form of Cyril Hicks was hunched over a table, working late into the night. There was an articulated desk lamp beside him, but it was dark, unlit, as he no longer needed the light. In the black, he ran the Midas Coin over the rasp, filing away a little more with each pass. All his life, Cyril Hicks wanted power, and now he had more than he had ever dreamt possible.

Chapter Twenty-Two

London, UK
3rd of January, 9:10 a.m. (GMT)

The small brass bell attached to Bliss Catering's front door rang as Martinez and Wilson crossed the threshold. The front was staged with cake toppers, table settings, decorations, and menus tastefully arranged to spark the imagination—this is what your event could look like if you went with Bliss.

A small bookshelf held binders containing hundreds of different options beyond those presented in the room itself. But the real star was the precisely decorated display cakes. Each showcased a different aesthetic from modest to outlandish. Regardless if the aim was for classic beauty, modern sophistication, or fanciful whimsy, Bliss could provide the perfect cake for all occasions.

"Welcome to Bliss!" a woman called out pleasantly as she came through the swinging door that led to the back. "What can we do for you today?" She was dressed in all white, the uniform of a baker, and the only color about her was the mass of ginger hair tightly constrained in a kitchen-approved manner.

Martinez stepped forward and pitched her voice an octave higher than normal. "Hi, I'm Charlotte and this is my fiancé, David. We're from the US and we're planning a UK wedding this spring," she began. Wilson gave a brief smile and nodded; they'd agreed that she should do most of the talking.

The baker did not fail to notice the giant rock hanging off Martinez's hand laced through her fiancé's arm. "Congratulations to you both! What made you decide on England?"

"I've always been in love with the country and culture. So much history, and the TV shows are just fabulous!" Martinez gushed. "And David travels here for business, so we can even write off a lot of the preparation and expenses."

Americans... the baker thought to herself without changing her fixed smile.

"A friend of mine used your company for a business meeting in London a few months ago and he really liked the food, so we thought we'd give it a try for the big day," Wilson added.

Pemberton beamed. Referrals were the highest praise in this industry. She had been hesitant to take such a small job, but her cousin convinced her it was a good opportunity to break into the highly competitive corporate catering market.

"Excellent! It's always nice to hear someone enjoyed our service enough to tell their friends." She offered her hand. "I'm Felicia Pemberton, owner of Bliss Catering, and I'll make sure you have a truly memorable experience as well. Let's take a seat and talk a bit about what you've got in mind."

She escorted them to a large white table and started asking the usual questions: date, venue, numbers of attendees, etc. Martinez fielded the question like a pro, and all Wilson had to do was chime in with the occasional "whatever Charlotte wants" and "Charlotte knows best." As Martinez spun tales about colors, themes, and how she wanted decorations that weren't going to clash with her dress, Pemberton was mentally adding up the itemized bill for all the American's desires.

If this is what she came up with on less than twenty-four hours' notice... Wilson thought as he excused himself. The restroom was in the back—the perfect excuse to nose around. He passed through the swinging door and walked down the hall. Through the circular window of the kitchen door, he saw a lone baker decorating a cake. Beyond that was a utility and storage room opposite the restroom. At the end of the hall was an unalarmed exit to the alley where the Bliss Catering van was parked. Wilson quickly circled it—it had a car alarm but it wasn't set.

He put on his gloves and tried the handle—unlocked. Wilson entered the back of the van and pulled out the loaded saltcaster tucked into his jacket's inner pocket. He waited to see if the blown salt would produce the same Dionysian signature, but the grains stayed still. *Nuts*, he griped as he dispersed the magic with a swipe of his hand and climbed out the van.

When he returned, Martinez was discussing the difficulty of finding a suitable venue that wasn't already booked. "There you are!" she called out to Wilson. "Felicia was afraid you had gotten lost. We were about to send a search party." Her smile was broad and bright but her eyes were sending signals. "She was just telling me all about the cakes they can make, and she can arrange a taste test for us if we have time."

Wilson planted a chaste kiss on the top of Martinez's head on the way back to his seat. "Cake before lunch—how can a man refuse?" he replied with a smile.

Pemberton politely laughed; cake tasting was historically a prospective groom's favorite wedding planning activity. "I'll be back in just a moment." She rose and headed to the back. The flawlessly executed cakes in front were works of art to display the finishing, but they weren't actually edible.

As soon as she left, Martinez whispered, "Took you long enough. I was running out of bullshit. Find anything?"

"Not in the delivery van, but there was someone in the kitchen so I couldn't salt there," he muttered as he pulled the loaded saltcaster again. He blew where Pemberton had been sitting to check if she was a magician, but the evenly dispersed granules didn't move, either. He brushed the salt off the chair and kicked it under the table.

Pemberton returned with a square board covered with thin rectangular slices of cake. "I kept your preferences in mind and added a few I thought you might like," the baker announced as she presented the board. Each slice was labeled, but Pemberton methodically listed off the flavors. "We have strawberry cream, white chocolate and raspberry, orange almond, hazelnut praline, tiramisu, carrot cake, red velvet, salted caramel, and mocha chocolate."

Martinez feigned excitement, and asked Wilson, "What's the flavor of that crazy gold cake your friend was raving about?" He shrugged and looked toward Pemberton.

She smiled. "That would be our 24 Karat Cake. We decorate it as a bar of gold bullion, dust it with gold powder, and stamp it '24 Carrot'—as in the vegetable. It's always a big hit and quite memorable, as your friend can attest."

"Do you use real gold?" Martinez asked luridly.

"Of course. It just adds a little glamour and decadence to dessert, don't you think?" Pemberton replied. She pegged Charlotte as someone who loved a little sparkle. "We can always do it as a groom's cake, or if you prefer to make it the main cake, we can have multiple bricks stacked to accommodate the large guest list."

While she was focusing on Martinez, Wilson knocked the sample board onto the floor, covering up where he'd kicked the salt and making sure to get some on his shirt in the process. He yelped as he pushed away from the table.

"Let me help," Martinez insisted, deliberately smearing a bit of chocolate just a little further with a napkin. "Oh dear, I'm afraid I'm just making it worse!" She affected distress, but Wilson could see she was having fun.

Pemberton took to her feet. "I'll get some help and we'll get that cleaned up right away." She dashed through the swinging door and Martinez genuinely smiled.

"Kitchen?" she guessed.

"Kitchen," he confirmed.

When Pemberton returned with cleaning supplies and the cake decorator from the back, Wilson announced his intention to clean up in the bathroom. As soon as he cleared the door, he darted into the kitchen and cast his salt. While he waited, he wiped off the cake and wet his shirt. If anyone found him in here, he could always say he was looking for some baking soda. He waited for the salt to move, but it didn't budge an inch. He kicked the salt harder than he needed to and returned to the showroom. Martinez—as Charlotte—was still apologizing profusely on his behalf, but most of the mess had been cleaned up.

"We'll have to take it to the cleaners," he broke the bad news to his fiancée.

"That's okay. We'll buy you a new one. I never liked that shirt anyway," she said flippantly.

It took fifteen minutes for Martinez and Wilson to extricate themselves from Bliss Catering with a second cake board, this one carefully put in a box to-go, and a handful of brochures. Martinez cheerfully promised to follow up once they had a firm date.

"Well, they definitively had the cake," Martinez voiced in her normal register as the door closed behind them.

"But there was no trace of Dionysus in there," Wilson remarked as he buttoned his jacket to cover the stain.

"Where does that leave us?" she asked as she pantomimed carefully placing the papers in her bag, smiling and waving goodbye through the front window.

He held out his arm to her to complete their ruse. "Now, we have a coroner to visit." She threaded her arm through his until they arrived at the car.

*****

Martinez looked up from the giant map unfolded across her lap and pointed to the unpaved road they had just passed. "I think that was our turn," she informed Wilson

"How would anyone know?" Wilson rhetorically asked. "You'd think we were in Italy, given the lack of signs around here," he groused. "There's a road up ahead. Let's check if it has a street sign before we do any more U-turns."

Getting access to Cyril Hicks was proving more difficult than anticipated. They'd stopped by his office, only to find it closed. They'd tried calling to arrange a meeting, but couldn't reach him at any of the numbers listed under his name. Then, they'd decided to go to his house and entered the address into their GPS. When it led them to the wrong place, they purchased a map—which was only helpful if you knew where you were and where your destination was. They'd been driving deep in the countryside of Buckinghamshire for half an hour and still couldn't find the coroner's residence. They could hardly stop and ask for directions if they wanted to fly under the radar.

The plan they had concocted was straightforward. If anyone was home, they were business journalists doing a biography of Carlmon Grollo for *The Economist*, an easily digestible lie given his recent death and the fact that Hicks was one of his initial investors. If the place was empty, they'd have the run of the roost to investigate.

A month ago, breaking into an empty house would have been unfathomable to Martinez. The FBI was one part of a larger criminal justice system. There were procedures and protocols to guide legal behavior. She didn't go in if she didn't have a warrant, or at the very least probable cause that a serious crime was being committed at that very moment. To do otherwise would make anything found inadmissible in a court of law, no matter how damning the evidence was. Those were the rules, and no one got very far if they didn't understand and obey them.

But at the Salt Mine, there was no search warrant to obtain or burden of proof for which one had to collect evidence. It didn't matter if things were obtained illegally, as long as it was reliable. And there certainly wasn't a judge or jury to dole out justice. All was permissible as long as disruptive magic and supernatural forces were contained, neutralized, or banished. There was no one to tell an agent in the field what was right or wrong. They had to know that for themselves.

Wilson had been keeping a close eye on his protégé throughout the case. It was his job to make sure she was eventually ready to do this on her own. Coming from the CIA, he was accustomed to a results-based job, but he recognized the culture shift she must be experiencing.

It had been an easy sell to break into Grollo's house because it was the scene of a crime and it obviously needed to be magically investigated. But this was different. All they had was a theoretical link found by the analysts—was that enough for Martinez? Could she do what needed to be done when push came to shove? If she had any objections, she hadn't said anything, but Wilson kept watch all the same.

As luck would have it, the next road did have a sign, and it proved Martinez correct—they had missed their turn. Wilson begrudgingly backtracked and took an unmarked gravel road through some scraggly woods. They traveled it for a good hundred yards before it opened up into a driveway.

For the price, they had expected a grand estate, but instead they found a late nineteenth-century farmhouse with modern additions. The old barn had been converted into a four-car garage with loft rooms above it, and the house proper had been expanded, doubling its square footage.

"It doesn't look like anyone is home," Martinez surmised by the look of the outside.

"We should ring the doorbell just in case someone is in the

back," Wilson advised. If it had been night, or they had hard intel that no one was home, he would have suggested doing a perimeter sweep and going in. "It becomes significantly harder to talk our way out of trouble once we break in."

Chapter Twenty-Three

Piddington, Buckinghamshire, UK
3rd of January, 12:10 p.m. (GMT)

No one had seen the Hicks family in a while, but none of their friends or associates were bothered. They were supposed to be out of town for a ski trip, and everyone was too busy with their own holiday plans to notice their absence on social media. The only people who had a clue that anything was amiss were the airline and the Alpine lodge, as the Hicks family had failed to check in. Neither company would raise an alarm; they simply kept their deposits and sold their spots once the grace period was over.

Anyone who stopped by the house would find it tucked away and tidy. There were no piles of uncollected post or packages, as Royal Mail dutifully followed their prearranged vacation hold. All the windows and shutters were closed and the lights were never on, even at night. But the house was far from empty because the mortal husk of Cyril Hicks stalked its shadowy halls. He was little more than a corrupted flesh suit for the being that now wore him. Hicks was still inside there, somewhere, but he was no longer calling the shots. Possessed by Buer, he could only watch as the horrors unfolded before his very eyes—which was the one part of his anatomy the demon had kept intact.

It had spent all night and morning filing away at the coin, adding to the growing pile of gold dust. It never dared shave more than half, lest it be irreplaceably consumed and fail to regenerate. It gleefully considered different ways of introducing it into the general public—which targets would spread the fastest, the farthest, and with the greatest effect. *And they say demons have no discipline!* it scoffed internally.

Quite pleased with its latest scheme, it decided to have a proper lunch with the family. Technically, it did not need nourishment, but it took immense pleasure in the macabre farce of a family at mealtime. Before it entered the dining room, it called out, "Honey, I'm home!" A vile chuckle echoed against the bloodstained walls as it laughed at its own joke.

It dutifully kissed the rotting face of Mrs. Hicks and patted Hicks's son on the head. His broken neck caused it to flop to the side. They were both quite difficult to maneuver in their natural state, but that mattered little to Buer. It had spent eons breaking human flesh and souls. It was nothing a little dismembering and rewiring couldn't fix when needs must. Occasionally, he would yank a string here or jostle a body part there and the movement simulated life with waggling fetid flesh.

Buer—in his Hicks suit—took a seat at the head of the dining room table, breathing deep the stench of decay and filth. It was finally starting to smell like home. It was about to perform a little panto show with the wired corpses of the maggot's wife and child when the doorbell rang. Buer turned what was once Hicks's head.

"Stay where you are. I'll get it," it perversely affected manners and rose to answer the door. It wondered who it could be. Everyone was under the impression that the Hicks family was gone on vacation.

The demon put aside such petty concerns. It was no matter; there was plenty of room at the table for guests.

*****

Martinez stood patiently at the door. She could hear someone moving inside and prepared herself to sell their cover story. When the door opened, the smell hit them like a brick through a glass window. It was acrid and noxious with a hint of sulfur, like paint thinner mixed with rotten eggs.

Wilson knew the stench well and immediately drew his Glock, but before he could bring his arms up, a hand lashed out from behind the door. With a flick of the wrists, Wilson's gun flew in one direction and he in another. He had just enough time to brace himself before he was slammed against the door of their rental car. Even with his summoned protections softening the impact, he landed with enough force to dent it.

Without hesitation, Martinez drew her concealed gun and aimed for where center mass should have been. There was not enough light to see her target, but she was confident it wasn't human based on the hand alone. It was covered in sallow green scales and had talons instead of fingernails.

She fired twice through the gap and was certain at least one, if not both, of her shots hit. Hicks felt the pain, but it didn't faze Buer at all. The demon let forth a cackle, scoffing at the feeble attack, and a chill ran down Martinez's spine at the unholy sound. Before she could pull the trigger again, she, too, was picked up by an invisible force and thrown like a doll twenty feet back onto the gravel driveway.

Buer was enjoying itself. It had broken its other toys too soon and was pleasantly reminded how fun playing with humans could be. His Hicks suit was getting stale, and it was ill-fitting at best. He wasn't even a real practitioner of the arts, just a flesh vessel for the Midas Coin's will. But here were two new humans for him to consider! As the demon sniffed the air, he smelled arcane ability—one of them was a magician. How delightful!

Back against the rental car's door, Wilson made a crawling dive for his gun. It was loaded with banishment bullets—if only he could reach it!—and it should take care of whatever the hell it was inside the house. He didn't even have to make a kill shot to banish the fiend, just hit it. Right before he was about to lay hands on it, the hand in the door rotated and closed, pulling talons to palm. Wilson felt himself pulled forward, like a tractor beam was emanating from the door. He dug in his heels and poured all his will into resisting it, karma be damned; it didn't mean anything if he became demon chow. Or worse.

The laugh that came out of the doorway was perverse and malevolent; none of the Hicks family had put up much of a fight, but this one was feisty! Buer considered how much more chaos it could accomplish possessing the body of a practitioner. It pulled out a second hand, this one covered in gray fur and tiny hooves at the end of each digit, and doubled down its power. It didn't matter if it drained Hicks to nothing in the effort; it was done wearing him anyway.

Martinez got to her feet and still had her gun, but she knew firing it again would be pointless. She saw Wilson's gun twenty feet away and scrambled for it. Buer saw her dash across the rocks, but was too busy acquiring its next host. It would deal with her later.

Wilson was slowly being dragged toward the front door, even though he was putting everything he could between him and the demon. The demon was besting him, if just barely, but his heart skipped a beat when he saw a third grotesque hand emerge from the door, twist unnaturally, and amplify the force he fought against. He was yanked toward the house like a water-skier when the line finally tightened.

Martinez grabbed Wilson's Glock, took aim, and fired

twice into the sliver of space between Wilson, the door, and the jamb. An inhuman scream wailed from the threshold, and Wilson fell hard against the gravel, backward rolling in the process.

Without moving her weapon or gaze from the blackness of the doorway, she called out, "Are you okay?"

"Been better. I think we've found our bad guy," he said, raising himself off the ground with a grunt and walking to her. "Can I have my gun back?"

Martinez put on the safety and handed Wilson back his Glock. "Next time, I get banishment bullets."

"Deal," he agreed wholeheartedly. He took off the safety and pointed it at the doorway—just because one fiend was banished didn't mean it was safe.

"Do you think anyone heard?" she asked as she pulled out her weapon and followed suit.

"Maybe. But we're a long way from the road. The next house has to be half a mile away and four shots in a rural community shouldn't draw any attention," he answered in a low voice as he approached the house.

He kicked in the door and dropped to one knee while they got their first good look at their assailant. The body on the floor didn't even resemble a human, much less Cyril Hicks. It had five goat-like legs spread out spider-like around a bloated pink torso. Four reptilian arms branched out from every side, and the head…the head made Martinez retch.

"Don't!" Wilson ordered. "Step outside, close your eyes, and count to ten."

She turned away, walked back to the gravel drive, and took a deep breath of fresh air. Once the…thing…was out of sight, she immediately felt better. She heard another shot inside, this time significantly quieter. Wilson exited the house. "He's finished."

"He was still alive?" she marveled, horrified.

"Yes. Trust me, no one wants to be trapped in a body after a demon's ridden through," Wilson told her as he went to the car. "Think the car company will notice?" he cracked a rare joke before popping the trunk. He rummaged through his luggage and handed her the box of banishment bullets. "Load up, we're going in."

Martinez felt like she had been promoted from the kids' foldout to the adults' dining room table at Thanksgiving. "How did you know it was a demon and not a devil?" she asked as she exchanged bullets.

"A person possessed by a devil doesn't change like that; they generally stay humanesque. But the human body simply can't contain the chaotic forces of demons. It causes drastic changes over time and you can get some really messed up bodies," he answered as he unearthed a circular piece of granite about the size of a quarter with a hole through it.

"What's that?" Martinez asked as she handed him back the box of bullets.

"A hag stone, although it doesn't look like the ones they sell to tourists. If you look through it, you can see things that you normally can't, provided something's there to see, of course," he added before pulling out face masks, toothpaste, disposable gloves, safety glasses, and four shower caps and four zip ties.

"You don't want to touch anything in there. If we had full bunny suits, we'd be wearing those," he explained as he started putting everything on. "If you feel like you need to throw up, just stop moving and close your eyes until it passes—that's usually enough to reset your system. You'll get used to it eventually."

Martinez started with the makeshift booties. "What exactly is it?"

"Aethermorphic feedback, like Furfur, only worse because… demons," he said, rather blasé. "They're always worse."

"Are there more of them in there?" she asked, tightening the zip ties around her ankles.

"There shouldn't be. It normally wouldn't allow anything else near itself, but just in case…" he said, patting his gun.

Once they had donned their protective gear, they reentered the house. Wilson checked the pockets of the body's tattered clothes and found a wallet: Cyril Basil Hicks. Martinez managed to avoid puking using Wilson's advice, but gave Hick's body a wide berth anyway.

The stench was another matter; there was something quite dead in the house, and it overpowered the stink of all the dried feces spread on the walls, and even that of the demon itself. She could only imagine how much worse it would have been if it wasn't January. She focused on the minty smell of the toothpaste she'd rubbed inside her mask.

Wilson blew salt over the twisted corpse and waited until a pattern formed. It was similar to what they'd seen at Hindon House and at Roberts's, but there were other elements as well. "There's more than one magical signature here," Wilson interpreted the salt. "This part looks familiar, but this patch is different. I suspect we've found our CEO killer, but the demon's innate magic is causing interference. We'll keep looking. Prepare yourself for the worst."

The fetor deepened as they walked into the great dining room in the back of the house. Hanging from repurposed electrical wires were two corpses, one of a middle-aged woman and the other of a young man. In advanced stages of decomposition, their bodies had been broken and reassembled. The lines attached to their limbs led to a pair of crossed boards above their heads—they'd been turned into life-sized marionettes, with fully articulated joints moving in directions for which they were never intended. Wilson took one look and hustled back outside to gather himself, Martinez only a step behind. "Holy hell," she cursed as a break in the cloud cover gave them a rare slice of bright English sunlight.

"Demons!" Wilson swore under his breath as he reset his system and cleared his lungs of the stench. "They leave a stain on everything they do."

Martinez nodded as she fought the rising tide of nausea and horror. She would never conflate demons with devils again. After a minute of silence disrupted only by their deep, steadying breaths, they returned and Wilson again blew salt, this time under the corpses. A pattern appeared, but not the one they were looking for. "That's probably the demon's pure signature. See how these lines are different from what we saw at Grollo's and Roberts's?"

Martinez tried to wrap her brain around it. "So they were killed by the demon, but Hicks magically poisoned Grollo and the other CEOs before he was possessed by the demon. Where does Dionysus fit into this?"

"I don't know," Wilson readily admitted. "But he had to summon the demon somewhere. Maybe the answer is there. Let's do a sweep, and start with the basement and the attic first. No one summons demons in their bedroom if there is another space available."

They systematically went through the house, and Martinez took over the saltcasting as Wilson had burned through so much karma in the fray. He reassured her she had plenty in the bank—she'd just banished a freed demon.

"It's got to be in the garage," Martinez surmised after they cleared the last room. They hadn't found any more signatures nor signs of arcane practice in the house.

"If not there, then probably somewhere in the woods,"

he concluded with a hint of exasperation. "Grab the keychain hanging in the kitchen and we'll check it out."

Keys in hand, they walked up the external stairs that led to a solid metal door. They tried several in the slot before finding the right one. The loft was a single room the size of the entire garage below. Rows of glass cases demarcated one part of the room while the other contained a summoning circle. A single wooden stool stood at the end of one of the rows of cases.

"Bingo," Wilson announced, homing in on the circle. Passing the cases, he noted they were filled with rare coins and other small valuables. "Look at that." He nodded to the summoning ring. "What do you see?"

Martinez examined the circle, sifting through her memory of Chloe's and Dot's work. "It's the circle from the *Lesser Key of Solomon*."

"Correct. And the target?" he coached.

She looked again, searching for the target sigil in the inscription. "Buer."

Wilson grinned. "Correct again."

"But something's not right," she mumbled and bit her lip in intense concentration. He'd seen it immediately but gave her time to find it for herself. "It's broken!" she exclaimed, pointed at one of the letters. "This ascender isn't touching the circle."

He nodded. "Even the lettering must be perfect. There are no second chances in our art."

"How does a lawyer in the English countryside get involved

in demon summoning?" she inquired, somewhat baffled.

"Anyone can practice the arts," Wilson cautioned. "And it looks like his interest in the occult was more than just a lark," he observed as he perused the tomes on the short bookshelf. Some of them were quite old. Even if they weren't esoterically significant, they would have been expensive to obtain. "We'll take these with us and let Chloe and Dot see if there is any merit in them."

Martinez blew another round of salt opposite the circle, resolving into the same mixed pattern—half Hicks, half demon. "Are you sure Dionysus is involved?"

Wilson nodded firmly. The Smile in the Darkness was terrible in many ways, but it was true to its word. He looked over the room and saw a worktable. "Try over there, but keep your distance," he suggested. She pulled down her mask just long enough to blow through the tube and the grains shimmied across the floor into the same signature found in Grollo's calligraphy drawer and by Roberts's hospital bed.

An interesting idea crossed his mind. He attacked it from different angles but it held up. "What if Hicks wasn't a practitioner after all?" he posed the question as he pull out the hag stone. Although it granted magical sight, he didn't use it lightly. Looking through the stone attracted the attention of fae, and England was crawling with them—that was the last thing he needed after an encounter with a demon.

He held the stone to his eye and did a quick scan of the cases.

The one next to the lone stool lit up like a tree on Christmas Eve, as did something on the worktable. He quickly removed the hag stone from his eye and secured it on his person. "Cyril Hicks didn't kill those CEOs. That did." He pointed to the case.

Under the glass was half of an old gold coin; the contours of the face were mostly intact. Wilson viewed it from all sides while it was safely under glass. "If I'm not mistaken, it's a Midas Coin."

She dredged up her ancient mythology. "As in everything-he-touches-turns-to-gold Midas?" she asked incredulously.

"The same," he affirmed. "There are six remaining that were minted with his face, but only one known to have esoteric power. It amplifies one's desires, but it's usually limited to whoever is holding it. Infecting others with its shavings via dessert is new. That's demonic creativity for you."

"That would explain the bizarre nature of the deaths," she concurred. "Wait, how do you know so much about a coin we just found?"

"Because it's one of the items that went missing from the Mine's vaults a few decades ago," he replied. "Don't worry, they've improved security since then," he added when he saw her consternation. "You know what this means? The magical signature we've been tracking down didn't belong to Hicks."

She followed his train of thought. "It's Dionysus," she said in a half whisper.

Wilson nodded his head. "Just wait until Chloe and Dot find out," he muttered. It wasn't every day a god's magical signature was added to the database.

"And Hicks never was a magician," she extrapolated.

"Very possibly. Enchanted items are tricky. They long to be used, so it would not be hard for it to convince someone interested in the occult to summon a demon," he explained as he cautiously approached the worktable. Wrapped in a white cloth was a considerable pile of gold dust and a small steel file. Wilson kept his distance, even with his face mask.

Martinez bent down and looked at the stylized face on the remaining half of the coin. "How did Hicks get enough gold dust to make all that and poison the CEOs without destroying it?"

"I'd assume it regenerates as long as Midas's face is intact," he wagered a guess. "But Chloe and Dot will know more once we get all this back to the Mine."

Martinez eyed the gold powder. "How do we do that without being cursed ourselves?"

"I have a respirator in the car. We'll put the coin, file, and shavings in a containment box and pack it in salt. That should be enough for safe transport," he said, grabbing the interesting looking books off the shelf and making a pile for the librarians.

"And then what? What about the crime scene?" Martinez wasn't sure how the police would explain what had happened when someone eventually wondered where Hicks, his wife, or their son was.

"Obviously, we're going to have to scrub it with fire," he stated without batting an eye.

"Arson?!" she blurted out in shock.

"We've got to burn it all down. We don't want demonic residue hanging around—it's quite dangerous in and of itself. But before we do that"—he paused with the first full roguish smile she'd seen from him—"it's time to loot."

"Loot?" she asked for clarification.

"We're going to torch the place anyway, so we might as well take the opportunity to supplement our income," Wilson explained. He was already taking the other rare coins out of their cases—the hag stone had shown him they were not magical and the way they were stored indicated value.

"Is Leader fine with this?" Martinez questioned.

"She's the one who suggested it. She keeps ten percent of whatever we take to fund the Mine and the rest is ours. And trust me, you'll want all those extra resources once you start getting into the difficult magics. Karma isn't cheap and neither are some of our accoutrements. I'd suggest grabbing the best stuff in the smallest package because covert space is limited and the things related to the case takes priority."

Breaking and entering, firing a weapon at an unarmed civilian, accessory to murder, arson, and now theft? she ran down the list of offenses she had once assumed she would never do. But the die was cast and she had already crossed the Rubicon.

As Wilson emptied the last of the display cases, her mind went straight to Mrs. Hick's jewelry box upstairs in the main house and she wondered if the Salt Mine had an unofficial fence.

Epilogue

Boston, Massachusetts, USA
7th of January, 10:30 a.m. (GMT-5)

Charles Winston Roberts took a shallow breath and blew out the lit 49 on the small cake. He would not be partaking this early in his recovery, but the fact that it smelled good to him when the nurse cut into the confection brought a wave of relief.

It was a small party: just his two oldest friends and his nurse. The doctors had already paid their respects and speculated that if he continued to tolerate thin fluids by mouth and keep up with intake orally, the IV could be taken out tomorrow. The road back would be slow, but at least they were all setting their sights on an entirely different destination than they were last week.

Roberts didn't know what happened. All he knew was that he woke up the morning of the 5th and for the first time in months, he wasn't thinking about eating gold. The persistent intrusive thoughts were gone and the energy he had spent in relentless rumination was freed. Suddenly, he was hungry, but not for gold. For food. Once his nurse was satisfied that he could handle fluids without risk of aspiration—Roberts would not feed thickened water to his worst enemy—he started with watered-down juice, thin broths, and Jell-O. Roberts spooned lime Jell-O into his mouth that watered for his birthday cake.

"I promise we'll make it up to you when you are back to your old self," Thibodeaux pledged between bites of Boston cream pie. She'd ordered it from the bakery herself—it was Roberts's favorite. She always gave Chuck a hard time about it—he had to be contrary about everything; even his favorite pie was technically a cake.

Roberts gave a weak smile but it spread to his eyes. "Emily, right now I'm looking forward to apple sauce and mashed potatoes. Michelin stars won't be in my future for a while."

"That's okay, Chuck, you know all the best places are booked out for months," Phillips retorted, pouring himself and Thibodeaux a celebratory drink. They raised their glasses and toasted to Roberts's watered down apple juice. "To miracles."

"To second chances," Thibodeaux added.

Roberts clinked his plastic cup. "To the people who hold on until the end."

*****

Detroit, Michigan, USA

8th of January, 11:00 a.m. (GMT-5)

"They're so boorish," he stated plainly.

"They never talk to us," she noted. "They play that infernal machine all day long."

"And beard oil? What kind of fool puts oil in their beard?" he lividly objected.

Wilson patiently listened as Millie and Wolfhard stated their complaints. The dust was thick in the attic of his old house, undisturbed except for his own footprints on the rare times he would visit. "But other than that, they're fine people," Wilson stated. "Have they ever come into your attic? Don't they leave the doors open so you can easily come and go as you wish?"

They looked embarrassed, in so far as ghosts could look embarrassed.

"You're just going to have to learn to tolerate them. The times move on, people become different, and we must all adapt, even those of us no longer living," Wilson reasoned.

"But we don't want them here," Millie whined. "They prattle on about nonsense!"

Wilson felt he was at an impasse. "Is there nothing I could do for you to make you happy?"

"You could make them leave," Wolfhard affirmed.

Wilson sighed. "Make you happy *and* let them stay?"

They shook their heads, even the little one who never said anything.

"All right, then they're gone," he relented.

"You're a stand-up man, Mr. Wilson," Wolfhard declared.

"Yes, you follow your word. That's a rare trait in these crazy times," Millie added.

"It was rare enough when we were alive," Wolfhard reminded Millie.

"That it was. It was rare then, too," Millie agreed, her wispy bonnet bobbing.

"But you have to leave them alone until they've moved out. Give them some peace," Wilson added sternly.

"Certainly! We're excited to see who you bring in next. A young family would be lovely," Wolfhard suggested.

"It'd be fun to play with a child again. They're so much easier," Millie cooed.

"I don't know if it will be a family, but I know someone who's looking for a place of her own, and I think she'd be a perfect tenant," Wilson said.

"Who, who?" Millie asked excitedly.

"I think you're going to like her."

THE END

The agents of The Salt Mine will return in *Feeding Frenzy*

Printed in Great Britain
by Amazon

65551495R00139